Dear Diary,

I've experienced many joys in the past few months, but none could compare with having my baby back home. Oh, Jake's a man now, but he's my youngest, and to me, he'll always be the baby. I've really missed him. Of course, he's come back on some kind of mission, but I'm going to do my best to convince him to stay. And this time, I wouldn't mind if his "case" stays around, too!

Being around Camille Eckart and her infant son, Jamie, seems to have changed my loner son. And I, for one, am very glad to see it. Who knows, with the rash of weddings lately, maybe Jake will be inspired. Families provide an anchor—one that would keep my son home for good. And with luck, I'll see a few more grandchildren before long....

Dear Reader,

There's never a dull moment at Maitland Maternity! This unique and now world-renowned clinic was founded twenty-five years ago by Megan Maitland, widow of William Maitland, of the prominent Austin, Texas, Maitlands. Megan is also matriarch of an impressive family of seven children, many of whom are active participants in the everyday miracles that bring children into the world.

When our series began, the family was stunned by the unexpected arrival of an unidentified baby at the clinic—unidentified, except for the claim that the child is a Maitland. Who are the parents of this child? Is the claim legitimate? Will the media's tenacious grip on this news damage the clinic's reputation? Suddenly, rumors and counterclaims abound. Women claiming to be the child's mother materialize out of the woodwork! How will Megan get at the truth? And how will the media circus affect the lives and loves of the Maitland children—Abby, the head of gynecology, Ellie, the hospital administrator, her twin sister, Beth, who runs the day care center, Mitchell, the fertility specialist, R.J., the vice president of operations—even Anna, who has nothing to do with the clinic, and Jake, the black sheep of the family?

Please join us each month as the mystery of the Maitland baby unravels, bit by enticing bit, and book by captivating book!

Marsha Zinberg,
Senior Editor and Editorial Co-ordinator, Special Projects

JUDY CHRISTENBERRY

Guarding Camille

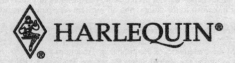

HARLEQUIN®

TORONTO • NEW YORK • LONDON
AMSTERDAM • PARIS • SYDNEY • HAMBURG
STOCKHOLM • ATHENS • TOKYO • MILAN • MADRID
PRAGUE • WARSAW • BUDAPEST • AUCKLAND

HARLEQUIN BOOKS
225 Duncan Mill Road, Don Mills,
Ontario, Canada M3B 3K9

ISBN 0-373-65071-X

GUARDING CAMILLE

Copyright © 2000 by Harlequin Books S.A.

Judy Christenberry is acknowledged as the author of this work.

This edition published by arrangement with Harlequin Books S.A.

® and TM are trademarks of the publisher. Trademarks indicated with
® are registered in the United States Patent and Trademark Office, the
Canadian Trade Marks Office and in other countries.

Visit us at www.eHarlequin.com

Printed in U.S.A.

Judy Christenberry has been writing romances for fifteen years because she loves happy endings as much as her readers do. In fact, Judy recently quit her job teaching French just so she could devote her time to writing. She spends her spare time reading, watching her favorite sports teams and keeping track of her two daughters. Judy is a transplanted Texan, who now lives near Phoenix, Arizona.

For Christina and Josh Willi, my daughter and son-in-law,
for their patience and support, and for Brenda Chin,
my editor, who always gives me a challenge
and hangs around to help me meet it.

CHAPTER ONE

DAMN THE WOMAN.

Jake Maitland regretted that thought immediately. It wasn't Camille's fault. She and the baby were the innocent ones in the chaotic events of the past six months.

He rubbed the back of his neck, but his gaze remained fixed on the woman who had become the center of his universe.

"Jake? Is that you?" she called softly, leaning forward in the rocking chair.

He stepped into the doorway so she could see him, knowing she would have covered her breast where her baby was nursing.

"Yeah, it's me. I was just checking on you."

"I'm sorry if he woke you. I'm afraid it will be a while before he sleeps all night."

Her soft voice matched her appearance. When Jake watched her, he always thought of the Madonna and child. Her beauty was enhanced by the sense of serenity that exuded from her.

He would never have believed the wife of a gangster could make him have such thoughts...ex-wife, he reminded himself.

"I was awake," he muttered, and drew closer.

She laughed quietly. "Too bad you can't feed him, then. I could use the sleep."

He held up his hands as if warding off evil. "I don't know anything about babies."

"And your family runs a maternity hospital? Please!" she protested, laughing again.

"I'm not part of the family business."

He moved past her to stare out at the darkness. No, he wasn't a part of Maitland Maternity Clinic. Hell! Until he'd come back with Camille, he'd barely seen his family in the last few years.

Yet when he'd needed a safe place to hide Camille, coming back to Austin—his home—had been his immediate gut response.

"Do you see anything?" she whispered.

He looked over his shoulder at the peaceful scene behind him rather than into the darkness. Mother and child. "No, nothing."

"Good," she said with a sigh.

He could tell she was rearranging her clothing. Then she lifted the baby to her shoulder and gently patted his back until a loud burp broke the silence.

"Talented kid." He offered the words with a grin, moving to Camille's side.

"Yes, he is." She started to rise, but Jake held out his arms.

"I'll put him in bed. You go on and get some rest."

"You said you didn't know anything about babies."

"I don't. But how come you're so experienced? This is your first baby."

"One of my friends had a baby a couple of years ago. I helped her out a lot."

"Well, I know enough to put this little guy in bed okay. I lay him on his back, right?" He'd heard that somewhere.

"That's right. Thank you."

"You need any help?" he asked as he headed toward the connecting door. After all, she'd only given birth a couple of weeks ago.

Again she chuckled. "I had a baby, Jake. I didn't break my leg. I'll manage."

"All right. Good night, then."

He firmly closed the door behind him before he gave in to temptation and assisted her anyway. He'd faced the biggest challenge of his career since he'd met Camille. For the first time, he'd let his personal feelings interfere with his job.

When he'd left Texas, determined to disassociate himself from his wealthy, socially prominent family and controlling father, he'd joined the FBI. His isolation only increased. The FBI didn't encourage fraternizing with civilians.

Jake had had no problem being alone. He'd hidden himself behind his badge. Women played an entertainment role occasionally, but never touched his emotions.

Until Camille.

Even so, he'd held himself aloof, distant. For six months, he'd pretended she was just another job, another assignment. He'd pretended.

That was the problem.

He laid the infant in the baby bed his mother, Megan, had provided. Then he stood staring at the sleeping baby in the pale glow of the night-light.

Camille had chosen Jacob as his second name. She'd said the baby wouldn't be alive if it weren't for Jake.

Well, hell, she was right about that.

James Jacob Eckart.

Not bad...except for the surname. This innocent baby's father was a vicious gangster.

Which was why Jake had figured he'd despise Camille. After all, she was married to the man. Well, had been married to him. By the time Jake had made contact with her, she was divorcing the scumbag.

Only her husband objected.

The baby squirmed in his sleep, and Jake gently rubbed his tiny tummy.

"It's okay, little guy. You're safe."

He'd met Camille while he was working the case against her husband. Without a lot of success. He'd trailed Vincent Eckart one day and discovered Vince was trailing a beautiful blonde.

Stalking, more like. When he figured out she was the man's wife and was in the process of divorcing him, Jake had been ordered to make friends with her.

Their friendship had gotten off to a rocky start. She hadn't wanted any new friends, particularly men. Finally, he'd identified himself as FBI. She'd insisted on seeing proof.

Then she'd cooperated, giving the FBI all the information she had. Unfortunately, it wasn't much. As soon as she'd realized the kind of work her husband did was criminal, she'd left him.

"Jake?" Camille whispered from the doorway.

He spun around. "What? Is something wrong?"

"No, but...you didn't come out. I was afraid Jamie was giving you problems."

"No. I—I was just thinking."

She crossed to stand beside him, way too close for comfort. Her rounded feminine body was clad in a lightweight robe that her warmth easily penetrated as she brushed against him. He tried to control the shiver that was his unwanted response. Just hormones, he told himself.

Leaning over, she ran one finger down her son's soft cheek. "I'm grateful."

"For what?"

"For the protection you've given me."

"I'm just doing my job." His voice was brusque, clipped, and he was afraid he'd offended her.

"And your friendship."

He wasn't comfortable with this conversation. In spite of the attraction he felt, or maybe because of it, he'd worked hard to keep his distance.

"I've been wanting to thank you for coming into the delivery room with me. I—I was scared."

He'd known that, and he'd broken his own rule. No personal involvement. And things had gotten very personal in the delivery room. He'd held her hand, caressed her brow, whispered encouragement. He'd held her son, then passed him to Camille's waiting arms, trying hard to hide the tears that had filled his eyes.

He cleared his throat now. Since then, he'd worked hard to maintain a cool distance.

"Just doing my job," he muttered again.

Camille raised one delicate eyebrow. "The FBI provides surrogate fathers? Amazing. Do they advertise?"

Her teasing sarcasm rocked him. He took a step back from the baby bed. "Camille," he protested, his voice carrying a warning.

"Why are you so afraid to be called a friend?" she asked. "Is it because of who I am? A gangster's ex-wife? Is it because, through me, Vince has hurt other people?"

"What he does isn't your fault," Jake assured her.

She stood beside him, her head down, saying nothing. Just as he was ready to ease himself away from her, she spoke. "Will you promise me something, Jake?"

"What?" he asked, his voice harsh as he feared what she might demand of him.

"If—if something happens to me, would you make sure Vince doesn't get Jamie? Would you ask your mother to find him a good home?"

"Camille— Yeah, I promise." He wanted to deny the possibility of her being hurt…killed. But he was too honest for that.

"Thank you," she murmured, and turned to leave the room.

He breathed a sigh of relief that she'd taken herself out of his reach. Out of temptation's way. It was just hormones, he reminded himself.

She reached the door and paused. "By the way, should I send the FBI a thank-you note for your delivery room duties? I really am grateful."

He ground his teeth, trying to think of an answer, but she didn't wait. The door closed quietly behind her.

CAMILLE PULLED the sheet over herself in the darkness and tried to fall asleep. After all, with Jamie demanding to be fed every four hours, she needed the rest.

But her thoughts remained fixed on the big man she'd left standing beside her son's little bed. Jake Maitland. It wasn't just that he was handsome, with a trim, muscular body, dark hair and the bluest eyes she'd ever seen. Bluebonnet eyes, she'd decided, after seeing the Texas state flower bloom this spring.

No, it wasn't his looks. After all, Vince was handsome, too. In a twisted sort of way.

And it shouldn't be the care Jake had given her, either, since, as he'd told her so often, it was his job.

When the FBI had offered her protection, she'd asked for Jake. She'd come to trust him—not an easy thing after she'd found out how badly she'd misjudged Vince.

Jake had tried to talk her out of choosing him. But she'd just discovered she was pregnant, and for the sake of her child, she wanted the best. And the best was Jake.

In so many ways.

When he'd identified himself to her as FBI, he'd suddenly become standoffish. The friendliness he'd feigned to gain her trust had disappeared. He'd let her see his skepticism when she told him she hadn't known about her husband's illegal activities.

Fair enough. She didn't blame him. She had trouble believing she'd been so gullible herself. But she'd been vulnerable, willing to reach out for warmth. Her parents had just died in an automobile accident, leaving her alone in the world. Most of her friends were married, and many had moved away from Washington, D.C., her home. Her job as librarian didn't lend itself to making new friends. The other employees were older, set in their ways.

Vince had come along when she longed for human contact. He'd teased her, laughed with her, encouraged her to rely on him. A month later, she married him, believing she'd found a new family.

Instead, she'd found a nightmare.

Vince wasn't a considerate lover, but she wasn't very experienced. She thought things would improve with time. But once the challenge of capturing her was gone, Vince changed. He didn't bother with charm any longer. Instead he issued orders. The first time she failed to obey, daring to question him, he'd slapped her.

Stunned, Camille had withdrawn. He'd turned on the charm again, teasing her into believing he'd had a bad day. It wouldn't happen again. But he pointed out that he wouldn't have had to slap her at all if she'd trusted him, as a wife should, and done as he'd told her.

Several other events alerted her to something rotten in the woodpile. She began to put offhand comments together. The second time he struck her, she waited until the next day, when he'd left the house. Then she gathered her belongings and as much cash as she could find, got in her car and drove away.

She should've known he wouldn't let her go so easily.

He'd tried sweet-talking her back to his house.

No sale.

He'd tried sex. Or, in Camille's mind, rape. She threatened to kill him if he touched her again. And she bought a gun.

He'd tried having a couple of his "employees" kidnap her, but she'd escaped and contacted the police. It was about that time that Jake came into her life.

She hadn't wanted to trust him. She hadn't wanted to trust anyone. But she needed help. After offering the information she had, she'd asked for protection. At first, the FBI hadn't thought her situation warranted any official protection.

Then, when she told them she was pregnant, they'd warned her not to tell her ex-husband. But Vince found out, anyway. She wasn't sure how. And he called her. He wanted the child, and he was willing to pay her a lot of money to come back to him.

She'd hung up on him.

For the next month, she was practically under siege. When the FBI finally offered her protection, after she'd thwarted yet another kidnapping attempt, she knew the man she wanted. Jake had been firm, patient and strong. He hadn't flirted with her, as one agent had. He hadn't been too familiar, either. A true professional, he'd only done his job.

And that's what he said he'd done the night Jamie was born.

Holding her hand, stroking her cheek, encouraging her when the pain grew intense. He'd even called her sweetheart, but she was sure it had been unintentional.

He'd done more than his duty. His duty could have been performed outside the delivery room, in the hallway. He knew Camille would have only the best of care at the hospital his family ran. His sister Abby was Camille's obstetrician, and Jake had total trust in her. But he had felt the need to do more for Camille. He'd been her friend, her strength, her rock.

And opened a Pandora's box of hope.

Because in Jake she'd found the man she wished she'd married. The man she wished was Jamie's father. The man who wanted nothing to do with her on a personal level.

She bit back a sob and tried to turn her thoughts to other matters. But since her world had shrunk to this remote cabin and Jake Maitland, controlling her interest in him had become impossible.

A reluctant smile was the high point of her day. A spoken word, not a sentence—Jake seldom used sentences—could stir her senses for hours.

His touch almost blew her away.

Fortunately, or unfortunately some days, he'd kept his distance. Though there were only the two of them in this small cabin on his friend's ranch, he'd managed to make her feel she was alone.

Until she'd gone into labor.

He'd rushed into the labor room with her, and from that point on had been the center of her universe.

He'd smiled, gently teased, given her the words she'd needed...and touched her.

"JAKE? It's your mother," Megan Maitland announced when she called the next morning.

With a grin, Jake said, "I know, Mom."

She ignored his teasing. "We're going to have a big family dinner tomorrow night. I know it's only a few weeks before Connor and Janelle's wedding, but I want to see all my family together again."

Jake frowned. Connor O'Hara, a Maitland cousin whose parents had been estranged from the family for years, had unexpectedly shown up last fall, much to Megan's delight. Jake didn't share his mother's enthusiasm. Something about his new cousin made him tense, and his professional instincts told him that both Connor and his fiancée, Janelle, were not quite what they seemed to be. They claimed to be the parents of the baby boy who had been abandoned at Maitland Maternity Clinic, but Jake had his doubts about that, too.

"Well, Mom, I'm trying to keep Camille out of the limelight. And I don't want to leave her alone."

"Of course not. I wouldn't ask that of you, but we'll have tight security at the house. Vincent Eckart would never be able to get inside. And you can bring that darling baby to the nursery. He'll be safe."

Jake remained silent. Megan's voice deepened when she said, "Jake, please. I've missed you all these years. I want you here, a part of our family. Don't disappoint me."

Jake considered his mother's words. He'd left Austin when he'd finished school and gone to the FBI, but he'd missed his mother. When he'd had to hide Camille six months ago, he'd told himself he was coming to Austin because it was the safest place. But after arriving and establishing contact with his family, he knew he'd come back because he needed to see his mother again.

He didn't want to disappoint her. And she was right about Camille being safe. It might even do the lady some good to see other people. Maybe it would even diffuse the sexual tension that was driving him crazy.

"Okay, if you'll do me a favor." Time to kill two birds with one stone.

"Of course, darling, anything," Megan replied promptly.

"Careful, Mom, you don't know what I'll ask."

"I'm not worried, son," she replied, her words full of love and trust…two things he wasn't sure he deserved.

"How about inviting Harrison Smith to your family dinner."

"Why?" she asked after a brief hesitation.

"He's asking a lot of questions about our family and hanging around the diner. He might be a private eye. I know he claims to be checking out the clinic for his daughter, but that doesn't take three months. I can't get away from here to investigate him and I want to find out whose payroll he's on."

"It would be rude to interrogate a guest."

Jake rolled his eyes. "I'm not talking about a spot-light and a straight-backed chair, Mom. I'll be sub-tle."

"All right, dear, but I'm sure he'll wonder why he's been invited."

"You'll come up with something convincing, Mom."

"Okay, be here at seven tomorrow. Oh, and wear a suit."

After his mother hung up, Jake muttered, "Damn. A suit." He'd hardly had to wear a suit in the past six months with Camille. He'd gotten quite used to jeans.

"A suit?" Camille asked from the doorway, a small tremor in her voice. "Are we moving? Going public?"

"Nope. My mother is the one demanding the suit. She's even more persuasive than the FBI."

"Oh."

He watched her hazel eyes darken with concern. "What is it?"

"I suppose Max will keep an eye on us here?"

Max Jamison was a local private investigator who used to work on the Austin police force with Jake's childhood friend, Michael Lord. When Jake had asked Michael who he could trust to help him out with Camille, Michael had suggested Max. Both Max and Michael, along with Michael's brother, Garrett, had been working with Jake ever since.

"Nope. Max'll be at the house. And so will you."

Nothing Camille had gone through since Jake first met her had come even close to producing the slack-jawed, stunned expression that was on her face now.

"I'll be where?" she managed to ask.

"You'll be at my mother's. We're having a family dinner."

"I can't do that. I'm not family." She succeeded in wiping all emotion from her face, giving him a blank stare.

Suddenly, several things fell into place for Jake. Camille had never attempted to contact anyone since she'd been in hiding, and she had told Jake that if anything happened to her, she wanted her baby adopted.

"You don't have any family, do you?" he said. He'd never asked her personal questions. It was his way of keeping his distance. He'd read her file, of course, so he knew her parents were dead, but he'd figured she must have relatives somewhere. Now he realized how very alone she must be.

She blinked several times but maintained her stoic expression. "I can't go to the dinner."

"I'm not leaving you here alone. We don't know where Vince is, but we know he suspects you're in the area. Do you want to take that chance?" Dirty pool, he knew, threatening her with her safety, but whatever worked.

"No! But—but surely Max knows someone else who could keep an eye on me."

"Nope. You're coming with me. The baby can stay in the nursery at Mom's. There'll be extra security. He'll be perfectly safe."

"Why don't you ever call him by his name? Do you dislike it?"

Her change of subject blindsided him. "Uh, I—I haven't gotten used to it." The truth was, he'd thought keeping the baby anonymous, nameless, would wipe out the memory of his birth, the warmth that had filled Jake when both he and Camille had held her son for the first time.

Damn it, this was his job. Nothing more.

Camille interrupted his thoughts. "I named him after you and my father, two men I admire." He opened his mouth to protest, and she held up her hand. "I know, I know, you're just doing your job." Then she smiled, a welcome change from the serious expression she usually wore. "Maybe Jamie will learn dedication to his work from you, if nothing else."

She turned away as if to leave the room.

"Do you believe your parents' death was accidental?" he asked abruptly.

She stopped but kept her back to him. "Yes. A drunk driver crashed into them, killing them both instantly. The drunk walked away from the crash with bruises. But it happened over a year ago. I hadn't even met Vince then."

Which, of course, explained Camille's vulnerability to Vincent Eckart. She'd met him only a couple of months after her parents' death. Jake wasn't sure he believed their death was an unconnected accident. Vince Eckart was amoral and wouldn't hesitate to eliminate anyone in his way. But saying that to Camille now would serve no purpose.

"No relatives at all?" he asked, moving silently to take her by the shoulders and turn her around. He figured the shocked look on her face was caused by his touching her. He avoided physical contact even more than personal questions.

"No relatives," she said quietly, keeping her gaze focused on her feet.

In an attempt to lighten the moment, he said, "Maybe I should loan you some of mine. They seem to be increasing at a rapid rate."

"What do you mean?" she asked.

"Every one of my siblings has married or paired off in the past year. I told you about them all. Then there's Connor O'Hara, my...cousin. And it'll only be a matter of time before babies start making an appearance."

"Be grateful you have family, Jake," she ordered, her voice firm. "They're important."

"We'll see if you still feel the same way tomorrow night."

"I will. But I won't be going to the party."

"Yes, you will," he told her, his voice firm. She had no choice.

"No, I won't."

"Why not?" he demanded, irritation filling him. What was wrong with her? Didn't she think his family was good enough? That thought was laughable. The Maitlands were sought out by everyone.

"Because I don't have anything to wear."

CHAPTER TWO

JAKE STARED AT HER. He'd expected fear, or something just as serious, to be the reason for her reluctance. But fashion?

Suddenly he felt as if he'd been hibernating for the past six months. Camille had been wearing maternity clothes she'd purchased just before he'd brought her to Texas. She hadn't had a lot, but never once had she complained.

Since she'd had the baby, she'd continued to wear some of her maternity shirts. He'd noticed a pair of slacks that he supposed she'd worn before her pregnancy. But her wardrobe was definitely limited.

"Why didn't you say something?" he demanded, frowning fiercely.

Her eyes rounded in surprise. "I haven't had a great need for a cocktail dress, Jake."

"But you've needed other things, haven't you? My sisters go shopping all the time. You haven't had anything new in six months." He should have thought of this before.

"Jake, contrary to popular belief, a woman doesn't have to shop every day to be happy. Besides, your sister Abby brought me a catalog when I was in the hospital and I ordered some nursing—some things.

And one of the nurses helped me pick out what I'd need for the baby.''

He shook his head. ''I'm calling my sister Anna. She'll get you a dress for tomorrow night. And I'll get you some catalogs so you can order regular clothes.''

The spark of interest in her eyes told him she liked his idea. The pleasure he derived from doing something for her alarmed him. It was just his job, after all.

Then she frowned. ''Can you access my bank account? I don't have any money with me.''

''I'll take care of it. You can pay me back when all this is over.''

A wistful look filled her eyes. ''Will it ever be over? It's crazy that I've been in hiding so long.''

''Yeah, it'll be over. We've got evidence against Vince now, thanks to some of the clues you gave us. And he'll face charges from the hostage episode at the clinic day care in April. All we have to do is find him. He's gone underground, but he won't have the patience to stay there.''

In fact, though Jake would never have agreed to use Camille as bait, that was exactly what was happening. Eckart was desperate to find his ex-wife and had trailed her to Texas. Jake was certain someone had passed on the information to Eckart and wondered if the leak had been instigated by his superiors in the FBI.

''Are you sure?''

He frowned, wondering if she'd read his mind. ''Sure about what?''

"I mean, will the government advance you money?"

"Yeah." The government…or his mother. How strange to have met a woman who was unaware of his family's wealth. He'd vowed never to marry after he'd discovered his first love was coolly calculating his inheritance. Between that and his family's social prominence, she'd intended to cut a large swath through Texas society.

"Can you call Abby? I don't know Anna and—"

"Abby stays pretty busy with her practice."

"I know that."

She should, Jake thought, since Abby had delivered the baby—Jamie, he finally acknowledged. "Anna plans weddings. She'll know where to get a dress quickly."

He reached for the phone, and as he'd expected, his sister immediately agreed to help. He handed the phone to Camille so she could discuss color and style.

"Jake?"

He whirled around to see what Camille needed. "Yeah?"

"Anna wants to bring some dresses out here. Is that okay?"

They were staying on Garrett Lord's ranch in a cabin remotely situated from the main house. Jake didn't want to risk Eckart following his sister out here in the hopes of finding Camille.

He took the phone. "Anna, can't we do this differently? Take a dress to Mom's and Camille can change when we get there."

"But it might not fit, Jake. Since she just had a baby, she's not sure of her size."

"She's wearing pants she wore before the baby— I mean, before she was pregnant. So the same size should do."

Camille tugged on his sleeve. "Jake, I—"

"Well, you are," he told her, anxious for this conversation to be over.

"Yes, but—on top I'm—I'm bigger."

Her cheeks were flushed, but Jake figured they were pale compared to his face. Damn, he didn't want to think about her breasts. But it was all he could think about now.

"Anna, bring the dresses to the main ranch house and we'll meet you there." He pressed the phone closer to his ear. "And don't tell anyone what you're doing."

"Of course not. But does Camille need anything else? I might as well pick up other things while I'm shopping for her."

Anna sounded amused, which irritated Jake all the more. He handed the phone to Camille with a gusty sigh. "Anna wants to know if you need anything else."

"Can we afford—"

"Yes, whatever!" He didn't want any more talk about Camille's body or her wardrobe.

Camille began a discussion with Anna, but a thin wail stopped her almost at once. "Oh, Jamie—"

"I'll get him. Finish up with Anna."

He fled the room. He'd much rather deal with a newborn baby than continue this conversation.

The baby was kicking his legs and waving his arms, his face puckering as he yelled. Jake sighed. He was learning how insistent a newborn could be. The first thing to do was check his diaper. Jake knew that much.

After changing him, Jake eased his big hand under the baby's body and lifted him to his shoulder. "Now, listen, Jamie, Mom's kind of busy, so you need to stop that yelling."

Much to Jake's surprise, the baby quietened. For a minute. Then little whimpers began to build. Panic filled Jake. What was he supposed to do? He drew a deep breath, determined not to be bested by a seven-pound infant. Even if he was a cute one. He cradled Jamie in his arms, then tucked the baby's small fist into his tiny mouth, hoping he could fool the baby into believing he was being fed.

The sucking noises were a dead giveaway. The kid wanted to eat. Jake was proud of himself for correctly assessing the situation, but he knew he didn't have the equipment for a successful resolution. Which, of course, brought his mind back to Camille's breasts.

Man, he needed some distance from his two captives! He left the nursery and returned to the living area, where Camille was on the phone.

It didn't take Jamie long to realize that his fist wasn't providing satisfaction. Just as Jake came into the room, the baby let out another wail.

"Oh, Anna," Camille said when she saw him, "thank you so much, but I have to feed the baby now. Oh. Yes, of course."

She handed the phone to Jake. He transferred the

baby to her arms, surprised by his reluctance to give up the warm bundle. Then he spoke to Anna.

"So we get to meet the mystery woman now?" Anna asked softly.

"Yeah, Mom insisted. But it's important that no one talk about her, especially to that pest Chelsea. Too many people know about Camille already." In the past year his family had been besieged by Chelsea Markum, a television reporter for a gossip show called *Tattle Today TV*. There was no way he wanted her to do a news item on Camille being guarded by the Maitlands' youngest son.

"You know we wouldn't tell her anything," Anna protested indignantly.

"I know, Anna, but this is a matter of life and death." He turned to stare at Camille, who'd begun nursing Jamie. Her eyes were shuttered, but her lips had tightened with fierce protectiveness. He regretted his words. But damn it, he'd only spoken the truth.

Anna made her promises and then asked him to bring Camille to Garrett's at four that afternoon.

"You can take care of it by then?"

"Good heavens, Jake, that's six hours away. I'm not going to hand sew the clothes, just buy them."

"Yeah, okay."

When he'd hung up the phone, he turned to Camille. "I didn't mean to upset you."

"I know."

"I'll keep you safe."

"Yes." She looked at her child, running her hand up and down his back in a soothing motion. Then, for the first time, she asked Jake about his care of her.

"Jake, why did we come here alone? Why don't you have a partner?"

This was the question he'd dreaded. He sat beside her. "Because I think someone is leaking information to Vince."

"Someone with the FBI?" she asked, sounding shocked.

"Maybe. You never told Vince you were pregnant, but he found out before you were even showing."

"Yes," she said, frowning. "I wondered how, but—but I guessed that he'd tailed me to the doctor's office."

"Maybe, but I was tailing you, and I didn't see anyone else."

"You were? Why? I had already agreed to cooperate."

"I know, but we thought you might need a little protection."

"I had already *asked* for protection," she protested indignantly, "and was denied!"

"I know, but my partner and I figured we'd offer a little extra, just in case. Nothing official." He didn't look at her. He didn't want her to know that her gentle beauty had already been tugging at his heart way back then.

He could feel her gaze on him, but he kept staring at his hands clasped between his knees.

"At least here I have people I can trust—my family, our friends the Lords."

"I hate the fact that I'm putting your entire family in danger!" Camille exclaimed. "Maybe I should just leave."

"You're not going anywhere. And my family's not in danger. Neither are you."

"But, Jake—"

"Enough! You need to think about the baby—Jamie. We've got to keep Jamie safe."

Her arms tightened on her little son, causing him to whimper in protest.

"Easy, there, you don't want to squeeze the stuffing out of him," Jake cautioned, grinning.

"No, no, I don't." She looked at the baby, then at Jake. "I have to change sides. I'll go to the bedroom."

He nodded, standing. As she left the room, he called, "Take a nap after you put Jamie back in his bed. You'll need your strength to deal with Anna this afternoon."

Camille paused and stared at him. "She sounded very nice on the phone."

"Oh, she's nice. But she's a whirlwind. She'll wear you out."

Camille gave him a faint smile and disappeared.

Jake picked up the phone again. This time he called Max Jamison. "Max, Anna is bringing some things to the ranch house at four today. Could you tail her, make sure no one else is doing the same thing? And plan on staying until she leaves? Great. I'll see you then."

While Max kept an eye on the ladies, Jake could drive into Austin and contact his boss from a pay phone. He suspected whoever was feeding Vince his information was keeping track of calls, too. Jake didn't want to lead Vince to the ranch.

Until the man was caught and placed behind bars, Jake couldn't distance himself from Camille.

Like a punch to the gut, the thought of Camille leaving, taking Jamie and disappearing from his life made Jake catch his breath. What was wrong with him? Of course she'd leave. Probably go back to Washington, D.C.

Where he lived.

When he'd left home, he'd sought power. His rounds with his father had left him feeling weak. He'd needed the discipline of the FBI, the authority…and the validation of being the good guy. Those early years, he'd felt he'd made the right decision. But he'd matured, and now he wasn't so sure.

He'd missed his family, his home, Texas. In particular, he'd missed his mother. While Megan Maitland was still young in spirit, still strong, she was getting older.

When he'd brought Camille to Texas, he'd noticed the wrinkles at the corners of his mother's eyes for the first time. And, for the first time, he'd thought about the future.

About leaving the FBI.

IN SPITE OF HERSELF, Camille began to grow excited about new clothes. She hated the maternity clothes she'd worn for so long. When she and Jake had disappeared in the middle of the night, she'd only been allowed one bag.

Jake had promised that her parents' house—now hers—and her belongings would be safe, but she had to travel light.

Since her social life had been nil, dressing hadn't been a problem. She'd worn the five outfits until she could no longer stand the sight of them. She'd also included in her suitcase a couple of pairs of slacks and blouses from her pre-pregnancy days, but the blouses still didn't fit.

She hadn't complained. She figured her life and that of her child were more important than clothes. But she had to admit she'd be thrilled to have something new to wear.

So why did she feel such disappointment when she realized Jake wasn't going to stay with her while she acquired her new belongings? If she were honest, she knew the answer to that question.

Over the past six months she had needed Jake to protect her physically, but she also had an emotional need for his approval. She worked hard to hide it. Jake wasn't interested in any personal involvement, she knew, so she didn't want to make him even more uncomfortable. Still, she couldn't help asking, "But where will you be?"

"I'm going into Austin. Max will stay with you."

"Of course. I thought—of course, we'll be fine." And they would, she knew, or Jake wouldn't go. But she'd been looking forward to having him see her in something new.

She blushed at the thought. It was only too obvious that he wanted nothing to do with her outside of their professional relationship. But his kindness, his big body, his warm gaze, all had become as important to her as fresh air. Once her ex-husband was put behind bars and Jake opened the door and told her to leave, she'd be lost.

She was in love with Jake Maitland. She finally admitted it to herself for the first time.

What a foolish, foolish thing to happen. An FBI agent and a gangster's ex-wife.

When it was time to leave, Jake escorted her and Jamie out of the house to his SUV. He placed a hand on her back to steady her as she climbed into the car, and she shivered. Admitting her feelings about Jake to herself had made his touch so much more intense. Good thing he kept his distance.

To distract herself, she thought about the last time she'd left the cabin, the night she'd given birth to Jamie.

Throughout her pregnancy, Jake's sister Abby had come to the ranch to examine her once a month, and then every week when she was closer to term. The plan had been for Camille to be admitted to Maitland Maternity under an alias once she'd reached her due date, but she'd gone into labor early, with intense contractions, and Abby had insisted Jake call an ambulance for Camille. Jake hadn't wanted to risk revealing their hiding place at the cabin so he compromised by taking Camille to the main ranch house, where the paramedics arrived and whisked her to the hospital. She smiled at the memory.

"What's funny?" he asked, looking at her as he drove.

"I was just thinking that even though I was at Garrett's house the night I went into labor, I was too distracted to even notice what it looked like."

Jake shrugged. "It's just a ranch house."

Knowing that was all she'd get from Jake, Camille asked, "What about your mother's house? Where is it located?"

"In Austin."

Well, that didn't tell her much. "Will Garrett be at the dinner?"

"Of course. He's like family."

"He's your cousin, isn't he?"

"He may as well be. He and his brother and two sisters were foundlings. Friends of my mother's—the Lords—adopted them. We've considered them family ever since. Mitch, my brother, was six years older than me, so I played more with Garrett and Michael."

"It must be nice to have so much family," she said wistfully. An only child, she'd always yearned for siblings.

"Do you want more children?" he abruptly asked.

Startled, she turned to stare at him. "I—I always wanted a big family, but—but without a husband—I mean, I wouldn't consider—without—" She fell silent, embarrassed by her incoherence. But his question had brought an instant image of herself wrapped in Jake's embrace, surrounded by several children.

He appeared almost as embarrassed. "Forget it. None of my business."

"How far is it to Garrett's house?" she asked, hoping the change of subject would help.

"About another mile."

"Then why did we leave so early?" she asked. It was only a little after three.

"I want us well in place before Anna gets there."

"Oh." She never questioned Jake's ability to protect her. After all, he'd kept her safe for six months.

"I called the house. Garrett's housekeeper is expecting us." He stared straight ahead as he drove.

"I've never met her," she replied.

He frowned. "We haven't exactly been meeting and greeting. But she's nice." To her surprise, he reached over and smoothed his thumb across her forehead. "Quit worrying."

"I'm not worrying," she hurriedly assured him. After all, she had confidence in him. But his touching her, even on the forehead, had her longing for more.

"Yeah, right. That's why you're looking pretty fragile these days."

Fragile? She lifted her chin. "I'm stronger than I look."

"You convinced me of that in the delivery room," he said with a shudder. "Thank God men don't have to have children."

It was the first time he'd voluntarily mentioned Jamie's birth. She closed her eyes as she remembered his arm around her, one hand holding hers, his strength pouring into her.

"We're here."

Jake's announcement had her popping open her eyes. To her astonishment, in place of the cozy little ranch house she'd expected, her gaze fell on a large, two-story home.

"My heavens, what is this, Tara?" she asked, thinking of the famous antebellum home in *Gone With The Wind*.

Jake shot her a surprised look. "Nope. Just Garrett's place."

Camille frowned as he got out and walked around to open her door. If Jake thought this house was normal, he must have been raised differently from her.

Not that she was penniless. Her parents' life insurance had left her with some reserves. And the government had promised to handle the sale of her parents' house and put the money in her account when she was ready, according to Jake.

But their house had been small, a Beaver Cleaver kind of house, not a mansion like this.

"Want me to take the baby?" Jake offered as he opened the door.

She nodded and eased the baby from his carseat and into Jake's arms, the contact between them sending shivers through her again. But she liked the picture of Jamie in his arms. His hands were so large, Jamie fit perfectly. Jake stood back so Camille could slide to the ground. Then he handed the baby to her.

When they knocked on the back door, an older woman invited them in. Jake introduced her as Mrs. Easley, and Camille thanked her for her hospitality.

She offered them a cup of coffee and they sat down at the kitchen table. The woman immediately began to ooh and aah over Jamie, winning Camille's approval at once.

Almost an hour later, Camille had finished a glass of milk, while Jake drank his coffee. They'd obviously come too early and had run out of small talk. But Jake was even more impatient than she was.

She and the housekeeper chatted quietly while she

fed the baby again, and Jake wore out a path through the house, going to the front to watch for Anna's car, then back to the kitchen to check on Camille.

"Jake, please, you're making me tired."

"I don't know what could've happened," he muttered, ignoring her complaint. "I tried calling, but she's not answering her phone."

"Jake—" Camille began again.

But the sound of a car stopped all of them. A van pulled into sight behind the house, and Jake opened the kitchen door, glowering.

As a pretty woman slid from behind the wheel, Jake shouted, "Where the hell have you been?"

CHAPTER THREE

CAMILLE WATCHED the other woman, wondering how she would react.

With hands on her hips, Anna grinned at Jake. "Hey, shopping is hard work. It took longer than I expected. Besides, it's just past four."

Before Jake could respond to that, the other door to the van opened, and a second woman got out. "What the hell are you doing here, Shelby?"

"Well, I feel welcome," the woman drawled.

Camille admired the women's sangfroid. Obviously they didn't bow to Jake's orders.

"This is supposed to be secret!" Jake practically shouted, frustration in his voice.

"Then you shouldn't be yelling," Anna said calmly. "Come help us carry things in."

Camille watched from her seat at the kitchen table, Jamie in her arms, as the three of them trooped through the kitchen and up the stairs with the clothing. She was amazed at how easy the two women were with Jake's anger. After several trips, Jake introduced them to her.

"Camille, this is my sister Anna and our good friend Shelby Lord."

"Are you related to Garrett?" Camille asked. She

noticed some similarity in Shelby to Garrett. A very feminine resemblance. Both women were attractive and fashionably dressed in tailored slacks and silk blouses, making Camille feel like the dowdy country cousin.

"Yes, he's my brother. I can't believe he didn't ask us out here before to keep you company," Shelby replied with a smile.

"Shelby, everything about Camille has to be kept secret," Jake insisted. "You shouldn't even be here."

"This is my brother's place. I come and go all the time. No one will think anything of it," she assured him.

Camille turned to Jake. His gaze reminded her to be discreet. Then he looked at the other two women. "Just fix her up for tomorrow night, okay? No questions."

"Okay," Anna agreed, smiling, but she sent a warning look Shelby's way before leaning down to look at Jamie. "What a sweet baby! May I hold him?"

"Yes, of course," Camille responded, "though, since he just ate, he'll probably go right back to sleep."

"We can only hope," Jake muttered, and received a glare from Camille for his efforts.

Anna smirked at her brother before saying to Camille, "We'll take your baby and go upstairs so *some* people won't bother us."

Her words didn't seem to affect Jake. His attention was focused on the road.

"What, or should I say who, are you looking for?" Anna asked.

"Max. He's going to stay here while I run into town."

Anna looked at her brother, a glimmer in her eye. "I'm sure you're going to give him a piece of your mind for showing up so late."

Jake ignored his sister's teasing. "There he is!" he exclaimed a moment later. As he headed for the door, he called over his shoulder, "I'll see you later, Camille."

She stared after him, missing him already, feeling a little unsure on her own. After all, he'd been with her almost constantly these past months.

When she turned to find Anna and Shelby studying her curiously, she shrugged. "Shall we go upstairs? I don't want to keep you any longer than necessary." That wasn't quite true, though. Female companionship, especially with these two charming women, was a welcome change.

"Don't be silly," Anna said. "We're delighted to meet Jake's mystery woman."

"I'm just a job for Jake," she hurriedly said, and followed the other two up the stairs.

Camille knew they'd carried in a lot of clothes, but she was stunned by the amount. Anna had brought a selection of casual clothes besides the dressier items. A linen jumper with several different silk T-shirts to be worn underneath was her favorite item.

"I love this."

"You have good taste," Anna assured her. "It looks terrific on you."

Shelby laid out several pairs of walking shorts. "You must've been hot lately in the clothes you have. It was much colder when you arrived."

"Yes. I had no idea I'd be in hiding so long," Camille confessed.

"Have you been bored?" Anna asked. "I don't think I could stand to be trapped in one place."

Camille thought back to the lonely days and nights. Jake hadn't been much of a conversationalist, though toward the end of her pregnancy, he'd opened up a bit more.

Then, when he'd gone into the delivery room with her, helping her through that difficult time, she'd thought they'd drawn closer. But she could sense he was pulling away again.

"I read a lot. And we have a television and VCR. Jake got us movies to watch." Though most of them she'd watched alone.

"Well, tomorrow night you'll get to socialize a little," Anna said. "Which brings us to what you'll wear at Mom's. Shall I show you my favorite?"

Camille nodded, and Anna unzipped a garment bag and pulled out a cocktail dress in pale leaf green. Its empire style relieved Camille's concern about her waistline, which hadn't quite shrunk to its pre-pregnancy trimness, and the frothy chiffon skirt gave the dress a certain grace and elegance.

Camille gasped. "How beautiful!"

"It will be perfect on you," Anna assured her.

Camille picked up the dress and gasped again. "But—but it's a designer dress!"

"Don't you like it? It's beautifully simple, such great lines," Anna enthused.

"Yes, it's wonderful...but expensive," Camille said, frowning.

"Oh, don't worry. After I talked to you and Jake, Mom called. She was afraid you'd have nothing to wear. She wants the gown to be a gift from her."

Nothing could have pointed out more clearly to Camille how far apart her world and Jake's were than his sister's casual attitude toward a designer gown. "There's no reason for her to pay for my dress."

Shelby chuckled. "Yes, there is. She figures she owes you for bringing Jake home."

JAKE WAS BACK in a suit and tie. And tense.

When he'd met with the FBI team the day before, while Camille tried on her new clothes, they'd assured him Eckart was staying well underground.

"He may even have left the area," Steve Parks, the team leader, said.

"No, he hasn't," Jake disagreed firmly.

"You've heard something?"

"No. But I know how the man thinks. He considers Camille to be his property. He won't rest until he has her in his control."

Even worse, Jake believed Eckart was filled with anger and revenge because he'd been bested by his ex-wife. His macho image had been damaged. He wouldn't rest until he had Camille under his power again. And heaven help Camille—and Jamie—if that happened.

"Come on, Jake. She's just a woman, not Cleopatra. No man's going to blow his entire life for a woman who doesn't want him.''

Jake sent a steely stare Steve's way. "Stay alert. He'll turn up.''

Now he waited for Camille to appear so they could drive to his mother's house. He wasn't comfortable about the drive there. Once they arrived and he had Camille inside, he'd feel a lot better.

He suspected Camille would, too. Ever since he left her at Garrett's house yesterday, she'd behaved differently. More withdrawn, quieter.

He should be pleased. After all, he'd rebuffed her early attempts at conversation. He'd ignored her offerings of friendship. For six months, he'd resisted her. And now that he wanted her to talk to him, *she* refused.

"Camille? Are you ready?" He checked his watch again. He definitely wanted them to arrive at his mother's early. There would be a crowd, since his family was large. His mother and father had had five children of their own plus his adopted siblings, R.J. and Anna. Then there were the four Lords, and Jake's cousin Connor and his fiancée.

And Harrison Smith.

Strange man. He'd come to town to check out Maitland Maternity Clinic as a possible place for his first grandchild's entry into the world. Not an unusual occurrence. The hospital's reputation drew the rich and the famous and extended far beyond the Texas border.

But something about Harrison Smith bothered him. He'd stayed too long, and his interest seemed focused on the Maitlands themselves, rather than the clinic.

"I'm ready," Camille said softly.

Jake looked up, still lost in thought, and was completely unprepared for the vision facing him.

His breath caught in his throat, and he thought he was going to pass out.

Dissolving into coughs, he bent over.

"Are you all right?" Camille asked, concern in her voice.

He straightened and looked at her again. Man, he was in trouble. He hadn't seen her in anything sexy before.

And she was right about her breasts.

The gown she wore was a halter top in some kind of shimmery green material that made her eyes look huge. It hugged her breasts and then floated around her legs, emphasizing every move she made.

Her silky blond hair, shoulder length when they'd first come to Texas, was longer now, but she'd swept it up on top of her head, revealing an elegant neck that made his mouth water.

"Jake?" Camille prompted.

"I'm fine. You look—very nice," he said, hoping she wasn't aware of the reaction those tame words hid.

"Thank you. It's exciting to wear new clothes. Anna even brought some things for Jamie. See, he's wearing a new sleeper." She gestured to the baby carrier where she'd strapped in her son.

"Very nice. We'd better hurry. Here, put these on." He held out a white shirt, a tie and a jacket.

Camille stared at him. "You're kidding, right?"

"No." This was part of his plan to protect Camille. "You're going in disguise."

She took a step back. "But, Jake—my dress."

"It won't hurt it." He didn't mention the fake mustache in his pocket or the cowboy hat on the breakfast table.

He draped the jacket over the sofa and held out the dress shirt he'd bought the day before, along with the rest of the disguise. "Slip your arm in."

With a sigh, she turned her back to him even as she stepped closer to slide her left arm in first. It was almost as if she were in his embrace. He drew a deep breath and was assailed by her delicate, provocative perfume. With her bare neck so close, he had to fight the urge to trace its graceful lines with his lips. Damn!

"I'm afraid I'll mess up my nails," Camille complained as she turned to face him.

He'd been relieved that the white shirt covered her alluring décolletage. Then he realized what her words meant. "You mean...you want me to button it?"

"If you don't mind."

Mind? He couldn't find the words to explain the problem, because he'd have to admit what touching her did to him. With his mouth feeling as if it were stuffed with cotton, he growled and reached for the first button under her chin. Not too bad, he assured himself as his hands slid to the next button. But the third button—that was the test. His knuckles skimmed the warm, soft mounds of flesh above her low neckline, and he suddenly couldn't breathe.

Camille jerked back, obviously uncomfortable with

his touch, too. "I—I think my nails are dry enough now."

He nodded, still unable to speak. His gaze was fastened on her slender fingers, the nails painted a delicate pink, as she buttoned the shirt.

He was relieved when the process was complete, and handed the tie to her.

She stared at him blankly. "I don't know how to do one of these."

"Do? You mean tie it?"

"Yes, that's what I mean."

He stood there, breathing deeply, trying to think. But in the end, he knew what he had to do. He slid his hands to her neck and turned up her collar, then slid the tie in place, its ends lying on her chest.

Clearing his throat, he ordered, "Turn the collar back down." After she'd done that, he said, "Take the ends of the tie and—" He didn't know how to tell her. Finally, he led her to the hall mirror. Standing behind her, keeping his elbows as far from her body as he could, he reached around her and gingerly picked up the ends of the tie.

Moving as quickly as he could, he tied the knot and slid it to her top button, all the time inhaling her delicate scent.

"There," he said, glad the tough part was over.

"I don't think this will fool anyone, Jake," Camille insisted. "My hair and face—"

He held up a hand, stopping her in midsentence. "This will help," he assured her, reaching into his pocket for the brown mustache, "and there's a hat in the kitchen."

Her hazel eyes widened, but she made no attempt to take the fake mustache. He swallowed several times before he stepped closer again. He peeled off the adhesive protector and pressed the mustache across Camille's upper lip. Her soft upper lip. Her kissable lip. Hunger surged through him.

She sneezed. "It tickles," she complained.

"That's what a woman says when she kisses—" He stopped. He didn't want to go there.

"Did you ever have a mustache?"

"Yeah, when I was younger and wanted to look older." And more in control. More macho, able to face his father as a man. Able to determine his own future and not follow in the traditions already laid down by his family.

But instead of facing his father, Jake had stayed far away.

CAMILLE WASN'T SURE what she'd said that had distracted Jake, but he appeared to be worlds away.

"Jake?"

"Uh, yeah, here's the jacket. You put it on and I'll get the hat." He hurried out of the room.

She took a deep breath and tried to relax. When he stared at her lips, only to check out the mustache, of course, she'd thought she might melt. All she could think about was him kissing her. How much she wanted him to kiss her. What kissing him would be like.

"Camille?" Jake said as he stepped into the room. "Is there something wrong with the jacket?"

Her cheeks burning with embarrassment, she

scrambled into the jacket. "No, it's fine," she assured him. And it fit, sort of. A lot better than one of Jake's would have. He was a big man.

He showed her a felt Stetson. "I chose beige so there wouldn't be a sharp contrast between your hair and the hat." Without waiting for her to take it, he put it on her head.

"My hair!" she exclaimed, reaching for the hat.

He caught her hands. "No, don't take it off. You'll have time to fix your hair when we get there. We'd better go." He reached for Jamie's carrier at the same time she did, his hands touching hers again. Jerking back, he said, "I'll carry him. We don't want to mess up your disguise."

She surrendered her hold and stepped aside. "Okay. Will—will your mother—everyone else will be dressed up, won't they?"

Jake stared at her. "Is that what you've been stewing about? Whether you'll be dressed all right?"

"I haven't been to a formal party in years, or maybe ever," she confessed, avoiding his gaze. And she'd never been anywhere with a man who looked like Jake.

He shrugged. "Hang around here long enough and you will. Mom loves dressing up."

He escorted her to the SUV and belted the baby carrier in the back seat.

Neither of them spoke until they reached Garrett's house and Camille exclaimed, "Look, there's Max. And Garrett. Are they going to ride with us?"

Jake slowed down. "Nope. They're escorting us. Garrett will lead, and Max will bring up the rear. The only tricky part about the evening is getting you to and from Mom's.''

''Oh. Has there been any sign of Vince?''

''No.''

''Maybe he's given up. Maybe he doesn't want me or Jamie anymore.''

Jake pressed his lips tightly together before he answered, a grim look on his face. ''No. He hasn't given up.''

His words depressed her, and she sank back against the seat, staring out the window at the passing pastureland.

WHEN THEY TURNED IN at the gate that protected his mother's home, Camille spoke for the first time since they'd left Garrett's ranch. ''Oh, my heavens!''

Jake gave a wry smile. The house was imposing. When he'd brought friends home from college, they'd been overwhelmed by the magnificence of his home. His girlfriend, the one who broke his heart, had reveled in the luxury of the place and been eager to move in.

Once he realized his girlfriend was only interested in his family's fortunes, he had decided he didn't want to be associated with such obvious wealth. He didn't want to be different from other people. He didn't want friends who could be bought with money.

''I thought Garrett's house was—impressive. But this... You actually lived here?'' There was astonishment in Camille's voice.

''Yeah.''

''Were you ever lonely?''

That unexpected question brought a rush of other memories. "Hell, no. There were seven of us kids, plus Mom and Dad and the staff they hired to take care of all of us. Both my parents were involved with the hospital, but they spent a lot of time with us," he remembered, his lips curving in a smile. That smile felt good.

Once his world had fallen apart with Susie's betrayal, he'd had some problems with his father. When he left home, he was determined to make it on his own.

And he had, but his childhood memories felt surprisingly good tonight.

Garrett stopped and got out in front of the house as a man in uniform hurried to park his car. He stepped back and waited for Jake's vehicle. When it came to a stop, he opened the door for Camille.

An appreciative whistle split the air. "My, my, my. You're a little, uh, unusual, Camille," Garrett said with a smile.

Jake looked sharply at his friend. Garrett wasn't one to flirt. In fact, he was a very private man. But he'd been friendly with Camille.

Jake got out and hurried around the SUV. Garrett had his hands around Camille's waist to lift her out, and Jake had to fight to hold back harsh words.

"Will you get Jamie, Jake?" Camille asked as Garrett turned to escort her into the house.

"Yeah, sure," he muttered. After all his work to take care of her, he didn't even get to escort her into the party? He was going to have a few choice words for Garrett.

Max joined him before he got to the front door. "Need some help with that diaper bag?" he asked, grinning.

Jake gave him a disgusted look and shook his head. "You'd think they'd make these things without flowers all over them. Jamie's a boy, too. He must be pretty embarrassed to have his belongings in this thing."

"I think he'll survive," Max assured him.

"Did you see anything?" Jake asked, turning to business.

"Nope. And I've checked all the staff and extras hired. They're clean."

"Good. While I look around, I want you to stay close to Camille." A sudden image of the way she looked beneath her disguise had him amending his instructions. "But not too close. And don't let Garrett drool all over her."

Max laughed again. "That might be the hardest assignment you've given me. Especially when she gets rid of that mustache. Good thing no one could see her clearly on the way in. She could never pass as a man."

"Yeah," Jake muttered. "Where are the guards stationed?" He had a picture of Eckart in his breast pocket. He wanted to show it around one more time.

Max gave him the information he'd asked for.

"Right. I'll be back in a minute," he assured his friend.

"You taking the baby with you?" Max asked as they entered the house.

Camille was waiting with Garrett in the entry. "I'll

take Jamie. I want to see the nursery where he'll be staying.''

''I'll take her to the nursery and somewhere she can remove her disguise,'' Garrett offered.

Jake gave Max a stern look.

Max chuckled again. ''*We'll* take her,'' he assured Garrett. ''I want to see the setup.''

Jake hurried away. He didn't want either man to spend too much time under Camille's spell. They might never recover.

He wasn't sure he would.

CAMILLE was overwhelmed.

She gazed around the high-ceilinged room at the beautifully dressed women, the men in their suits, and felt as if she'd stepped into another world. Megan Maitland, an elegant and gracious woman, had introduced her to each of her children and their spouses.

The woman was well loved by her family.

Now she arrived at Camille's side, a beaming smile on her face. ''Camille, dear, let me present my nephew, Connor O'Hara. I wish you could meet his fiancée, Janelle, but unfortunately she's under the weather and couldn't join us.''

''Oh, I'm so sorry,'' Camille said. ''But I'm pleased to meet you, Connor. It's so wonderful that you and your family have managed to find each other after all these years.''

Megan's nephew was good-looking in a rugged way, but when he took her hand, his lecherous gaze roved over her. ''Yes, it is, isn't it?''

Camille wanted to like everything about the Maitland family. After all, this was Jake's family, and every member she'd met had been charming.

Everyone but Connor.

Something about him bothered her, and she tugged her hand away. A strong arm slid around her, and she jerked in surprise as she realized Jake had joined them. "Connor, Mom," he said, acknowledging the other two.

"There you are, darling," Megan said, smiling at her youngest son.

"Yes, Mom, here I am. Connor, where's Janelle? I haven't seen her."

A flash of jealousy went through Camille. Did Jake have a special interest in the absent woman?

"She's laid up with a cold and running a fever, so she wanted to stay in bed tonight, not take any chances."

The man sent a suffering look Megan's way, and she patted him on the arm.

"She made the right decision, though of course we miss her," Megan assured Connor. Then she turned to Camille. "Did you see Chase when you took your baby upstairs?"

Jake had told Camille about Connor and Janelle's little boy, Chase. For reasons Camille didn't know, Janelle had abandoned the baby on the clinic steps the previous fall. Then in January she'd shown up to claim her child, but he was still in Megan's care.

"Yes, I did," Camille said with a smile. "He's a handsome boy, and big for his age."

"Yes, he is, isn't he?" Megan agreed, sounding like a doting great-aunt.

Camille had been intimidated by Megan's appearance when she'd first met her, but then she'd discovered the warm, loving woman beneath the expensive attire. No wonder all of Megan Maitland's children adored her.

"What did you name your little boy?" Megan asked.

"James Jacob," Camille said, not thinking about the speculation the name might cause. Jake's hand squeezed her waist in warning.

"After Jake?" his mother asked in surprise.

"Um, well, Jake has helped me a great deal and—and his name went well with my father's."

Connor gave a harsh laugh. "I heard that my cousin was quite a stud, but I didn't know—"

"Connor!" Megan snapped, an air of command in her voice for the first time.

He sobered at once and offered an apology.

Jake seemed distracted, however, his gaze fixed on something or someone over his mother's shoulder. "I believe you have a late guest, Mom."

She turned to look, then said, "Of course. Mr. Smith. If you'll excuse me, children, I'll go greet him."

"Who's that?" Connor asked, frowning.

Camille could feel the tension in Jake and knew he had some kind of interest in the man who had just arrived. She wondered if he had any connection to her ex-husband, but instantly dismissed that idea. Jake wouldn't have allowed him to be invited to his mother's house had that been the case.

"A man who's checking out the hospital for his

grandchild's birth. Mom thought he might enjoy meeting the family.''

Camille studied Jake's face. His explanation was reasonable enough, she supposed, but something about his intensity alarmed her.

"I thought it was just supposed to be family," Connor grumbled. "Though I suppose since the Lords are here, there's no reason—"

"The Lords *are* part of our family, Connor," Jake corrected. "I'd suggest you not make that mistake in front of Mom."

The man glowered at Jake, then tipped his glass to swallow the last of his drink. He signaled a waiter and exchanged his empty glass for another flute of champagne. "Aren't you two drinking?" he asked, gesturing to the waiter's almost full tray.

Camille lifted her glass of club soda. "I have something, thank you."

Jake didn't bother with excuses. He shook his head at the waiter and continued to keep his eye on the new guest.

A couple of minutes later, Megan approached them, a very handsome dark-haired man at her side. "Mr. Smith, I'd like you to meet my nephew, Connor O'Hara, and—"

Camille had been studying the new arrival as Megan made the introduction. When she gave Connor's name, the man whitened, all blood draining from his face, and Camille wondered if he would faint.

Jake grabbed his arm. "What the hell is going on?"

CHAPTER FOUR

JAKE SLIPPED a hand beneath Smith's arm to support him, afraid he might pass out. Instead, Smith squared his shoulders and shrugged off Jake's hold.

"Are you all right?" Camille asked, leaning toward him.

Jake recognized his instinctive urge to come between Camille and the stranger, but squelched it at once. There was no need to protect her. She was safe here.

"My heavens," Megan exclaimed, looking at Harrison Smith. "Are you ill?"

"Yes! Yes, I just got over a bad bout with the flu," he replied, a little too quickly, Jake decided. "I thought I was fully recovered but I guess I've had too long a day."

Connor shrugged. "You probably should go home. Put your feet up."

Jake smiled at his mother. "I'll take Mr. Smith to the study and let him rest. He'll probably be okay in a few minutes." He didn't want his opportunity to question the man to disappear. Especially now.

"I'll find him something to eat," Camille added. She smiled sympathetically at Smith, and Jake felt the stirrings of jealousy. What was wrong with him? She was only trying to be helpful.

"Thank you. I'd appreciate it," Smith murmured, returning Camille's smile.

For a prospective grandfather, Smith's smile was a little too appreciative of Camille's concern, Jake thought. Placing his hand on Smith's shoulder, he directed him away from her. As he did so, he caught Michael Lord's gaze and nodded toward Camille.

"I hope you're able to stay, Mr. Smith," Megan said, her social graces intact, as always. "Maybe if you rest until dinner, you'll feel better."

"Thank you," he murmured.

Camille flagged down a waiter and conferred with him as Jake led Smith toward the study. She'd be safe, he assured himself as he caught sight of Michael heading toward her. Nothing could happen to her while he questioned the guest.

Once they reached the study, Smith stepped away from Jake.

"Thank you for your support. I'm feeling much better now. If you want to return to the party, I'll stay here for a few minutes."

Jake stuck his hands into his pants pockets and shrugged. "I've been to too many of these parties. I'd just as soon have a break, too."

"I wouldn't want to upset your mother by keeping her youngest away from the party," Smith said with a slight smile.

Jake studied him. "How did you know I was the youngest?"

Smith didn't flinch or look surprised by his question. "I think it's common knowledge. You and your sister Anna are the only ones not involved in the hospital. I suppose that fact made you stand out." He chose one of the large leather chairs tucked in a corner of the shadowy room, away from the glow of the lamp.

Jake paced around the room. "So, I understand your daughter is expecting."

"Yes."

"Where is she?"

"At home. In Montana." He kept his gaze fixed on the cuff of his shirt, which he straightened with his opposite hand.

"And her husband?"

One eyebrow slid up, reminding Jake of Megan when one of her children had challenged her. He almost grinned, then regained control of himself.

"Are you implying I'm interfering with my daughter's life?"

Jake didn't back down. "I just know if my wife was having a child, I'd be the one making the decisions about the birth, not my father-in-law." Memories of Jamie's birth flooded him. Jamie wasn't his child, but Jake had been there for Camille.

"You've never—" Smith began, when the door, which Jake had closed, swung open.

Camille entered with a tray filled with hors d'oeuvres and glasses of club soda. She was followed by Michael. Jake wasn't surprised. He and Michael had discussed Harrison Smith and his probing questions. As head of security for Maitland Maternity, Michael had a few questions of his own.

He strode across the room and offered his hand to Smith. Camille hurried in his footsteps to put her tray on a table beside Smith's chair.

"I think if you'll eat a little, Mr. Smith, you'll feel better," she said, smiling at him.

Jake couldn't help himself. He crossed the room and took Camille's arm. "You'd better go back to the party."

Camille raised an eyebrow. "I don't think I'll be missed, except by your cousin Connor. He seems, uh, eager to get to know me."

Jake had recognized the leer on Connor's face. He'd told himself he was being hypersensitive, but the thought of sending Camille back to the party without his protection wasn't a happy thought.

"Thank you for the food," Smith said to Camille. "I promise I'll be fine after a few minutes' rest and these snacks. I don't want to keep any of you from the party."

Jake stubbornly refused to be dismissed. "Look at it as an opportunity to get even more information about the hospital, Mr. Smith. After all, Michael is head of security. He can answer any questions you might have in that area."

Smith studied Jake, as if questioning his words, before he smiled at Camille. "I think I've already asked too many questions about the hospital. I believe Mr. Maitland thinks I'm obsessive about my daughter's welfare."

Camille smiled in return. "Having a baby, even a grandbaby, is an important event. I admire your concern."

Smith nodded. "I have to admit, I find the unusual story of your cousin's return to the family fold more interesting," he said, looking at Jake. "It was a topic of conversation for a while at the diner near the clinic."

Jake wasn't surprised. His suspicions were confirmed. The man was here to check out his family. Jake wouldn't allow anyone to threaten his family if he could help it. Even if it meant forgetting the graciousness his mother always extended to guests. "I thought you might."

Smith narrowed his gaze. "Why would you say that?"

"Because it was the introduction to Connor that brought on your weakness, wasn't it? Not the flu."

"Jake!" Camille exclaimed. "You sound like you're accusing Mr. Smith of something. It's perfectly normal to feel weak after a bout with the flu."

Jake kept his gaze on the man. "But he's been here for almost three months, Camille, and the flu doesn't seem to have prevented him from snooping into my family's private affairs."

"I'm sorry if my questions have bordered on the personal," Smith said.

Michael got down to business, ignoring their sparring. "Why are you interested in Connor's story?"

That eyebrow slipped up again. "It's an intriguing story. Dramatic."

"Yes, it is," Jake agreed, "but not enough to cause you to send all the blood to your feet. Unless that's a common occurrence in your life."

Camille tried to pull free from his hold on her arm,

but Jake tightened his fingers. "Jake, I don't understand why you're—"

"I think Mr. Smith understands. He's hiding something."

A small smile played across the man's lips, and Jake was shocked to discover an urge to return that smile. He liked the man's cool demeanor. A lot more than he liked anything about Connor.

To Jake's surprise, after staring first at him and then Michael, Camille looked at Smith. "I don't know if Jake's right or not, Mr. Smith, but I can tell you that both these men are trustworthy. Jake has kept me safe over the past few months and he even helped me get through the birth of my child. And Michael upped the security at the clinic while I was there to protect me from my ex-husband. If you have a problem, you can trust these men with it."

Jake wrapped his arm around her shoulders, dropping a kiss on her forehead. He wasn't thrilled with her indiscretion in revealing her situation to Smith, but he couldn't help being pleased by her praise.

He looked at Smith and found his gaze fastened on the two of them. But when the man spoke, it was to Camille. "He helped you with your baby's delivery? I didn't know he was medically trained."

Camille's cheeks blazed with embarrassment. "No, he—"

Jake intervened. "I managed the hand-holding duties, Smith, not the delivery."

"Ah. And here I was thinking about hiring you to help deliver my grandchild."

Michael spoke before Jake could. "Let's cut to the

chase, Mr. Smith. There is no grandchild. There is no daughter. In fact, I'm not sure even *you* exist.''

''You got reports back?'' Jake asked. He knew Michael had sought some information on Smith after he started asking questions.

''You do background checks on all potential clients?'' Smith asked. ''You must stay very busy.''

''Cut line, Smith,'' Jake insisted, dropping his arm from Camille's shoulders and stepping closer. ''Your questions were about the family more than they were about the facilities. What do you want?''

He felt Camille's grip on his arm this time, as if she were trying to hold him back.

''He hasn't done anything wrong by asking questions, has he, Jake?'' she objected.

Jake didn't respond. His gaze remained fixed on Smith's face as he waited for his answer.

When the man reached for his back pocket, both Jake and Michael moved, pinning his arms to the chair. Camille gasped at the sudden action.

''Easy, guys,'' Smith said, keeping his voice under control. ''I was going to get my wallet, to show you identification.''

The two men pulled him to his feet. While Michael held his arms, Jake frisked the man. The only thing he found, other than keys, was a wallet in the back right pocket. Jake eased it free and held it out to the man.

Michael released Smith's arms, but he stood at his side, ready to act again if necessary.

It was to Camille that Smith spoke. ''They're very efficient, aren't they?''

Camille smiled. "Very."

Smith's features turned serious as he drew a driver's license from beneath the one bearing his name.

"Two drivers' licenses?" Jake demanded.

"Yeah. One for Harrison Smith, a fake, and one of my own." He handed it to Jake.

Jake stared at it, unable to believe his eyes.

Connor O'Hara.

CAMILLE COULDN'T help herself. She leaned closer to read the license. "Connor O'Hara?" she exclaimed, staring at the man.

"What?" Michael cried as he, too, crowded in to see the license.

Jake stared at Smith. "Explain."

His crisp order released Camille from her frozen state. She moved to the nearest chair and sank into it. "I don't understand," she whispered.

"Neither do we," Michael assured her, "but Mr. Smith is going to explain. Aren't you?" The insistence in his voice indicated his words were more than a suggestion.

"Yeah, I'll explain. Whether you believe me or not is up to you. Why don't you sit down? It's not a brief story." Smith sank into his seat next to Camille.

Jake stepped to Camille's chair. "You come here with me," he ordered, gesturing to the identical pair of chairs facing Smith.

"Why?" she asked, frowning. What difference did her choice of seat make?

"So I can protect you. Michael will sit by Smith."

"O'Hara," the man murmured, staring at Jake. "Your cousin."

As if his words were a surprise, as if he hadn't yet made the connection that this man was his kin, Jake stared at him guardedly. "Maybe," he returned.

Smith smiled. "Glad to know I have cautious relatives."

Camille felt Jake tense. To distract him, she stood and crossed to the chairs he'd indicated, snagging his hand as she went. "Come on, Jake, sit down so he can tell us what's going on."

"Caution is inevitable," Michael said quietly, "when wealth and notoriety are involved."

"Yes," the man agreed. "Well, I'm not sure where to begin, but I suppose with my parents' feud with my mother's family, the Maitlands. We had no contact with them. But a year after my mother's death, actually a couple of months after the anniversary of her death, I received...a letter from her lawyers. She'd written it shortly before she died, urging me to contact her family. I was...naturally leery of doing so. The family had caused her a lot of pain." He paused, as if waiting for a response.

"The other Connor told us all this," Jake said with a growl.

Camille squeezed his hand slightly, drawing his gaze. "He hasn't finished," she said quietly.

The man sighed. "Look, I decided to come down here to find out about—about the family. It was a shock to meet the man impersonating me, that's all."

Camille watched Michael and Jake exchange a

glance. She smiled at Smith. "Well, my vote is for you. I don't much care for the other Connor."

"It's not a matter of voting," Jake said harshly. "If you're Connor, who is the other man?"

Smith shrugged. "I have no idea."

"And what about Janelle and the baby?" Michael added.

The man started to shrug again, but he stopped and leaned forward. "Janelle? Did you say Janelle?"

"Yeah," Jake returned. "Do you know her?"

"A woman by that name worked as my mother's maid. Janelle Davis, her name was. She left after Mother's death, when I sold the place."

"Maybe that explains how she found out about your connection to the Maitlands," Camille began. "I mean, she might have been trying to get a better future for her baby, once she found out she was pregnant."

"Maybe," Smith agreed, nodding in a contemplative manner.

"But what about Chase?" Camille asked. "He isn't—he's not your child, is he?"

"Not if the baby is Janelle's," he replied, disdain in his voice. "She worked for me. I'd never..." His face turned red. Then he said, "I had no personal relationship with Janelle."

"Why are you embarrassed?" Jake persisted, leaning forward.

"I don't like being the subject of such speculations," the man said, clearly having recovered his composure.

Michael and Jake exchanged a look Camille

couldn't interpret. Her hand involuntarily squeezed Jake's as she said, "I believe him."

Jake turned to look at her, a frown on his face. "Why?"

She shrugged. "Women's intuition?"

Michael stepped forward. "What do you know about Sara, the waitress at Austin Eats?"

Jake stared at Michael. "Why'd you ask him that?"

"She's the other mystery around here," Michael said, shrugging. "I just thought there might be some connection. I don't believe in coincidence."

Camille had been watching the man, Smith or Connor, when Michael asked his question. Though he'd covered it up quickly, she'd seen the recognition in his eyes. She hated to betray him, but she put a hand on Jake's arm. "He knows her."

All three men stared at her. Before Jake could again question her, the man sighed. Then he said, "Yes, I know her. She once worked for me, too. Her real name is Lacy Clark."

Michael's words held a hint of sarcasm. "Pretty amazing that two of your former employees in Montana should turn up here in Austin. Do you think this Lacy was working with Janelle?"

Pain shadowed Smith's eyes. "I don't know. And they both worked for me in the Panhandle. I sold that place after my mother died and moved to Montana."

A knock on the study door before it opened startled everyone. Megan stuck her head around the door. "How are you feeling, Mr. Smith? We're serving dinner in fifteen minutes. I do hope you'll join us."

While she spoke, her gaze darted back and forth among the three men.

"Thank you, Mrs. Maitland," the man said, managing a smile. "I'm feeling much better." He paused to look at Jake and Michael, as if asking what he should do.

"Mr. Smith just said he was looking forward to dinner, Mrs. Maitland," Camille answered, hoping she'd covered the awkward pause. "I'd love to have him sit with me, since neither of us knows many people here."

Megan didn't look satisfied, but she graciously agreed. "Of course, Camille, dear, though I hope you don't feel like a stranger among us."

"Camille will be sitting with me." Jake ground out the words as he glared at Camille.

Megan smiled again. "My, my, you're popular tonight, Camille. Fortunately, there will be two seats beside you. I'll go arrange the place cards."

"Thank you," Camille said with a nod.

As soon as Megan had closed the door, they all let out a sigh.

"Do we tell your mother?" Michael asked.

"No!" both Jake and Smith said.

Then they stared at each other.

"Why don't *you* want her to know?" Jake demanded.

The man leaned back in the chair. "Because from what little I've seen of my—Mrs. Maitland, she appears to be utterly thrilled with Connor's return. I don't think she could hide her disappointment if she learned he is a con artist. And that might alert Janelle and her partner that they're in danger.''

Jake and Michael nodded. Then Jake said, "You're right, but that doesn't mean we've accepted your story. What about the birthmark?''

The man looked confused. "What birthmark?''

"Connor has a half-moon birthmark on his stomach, and so does Chase,'' Jake told him.

Smith shook his head. "No...I have no birthmarks.''

There was a tense silence, then Camille spoke. "I know it's none of my business,'' she said, "but did the other Connor have any proof of identity?''

"He had a driver's license with that name and his picture,'' Michael said. "And Megan said he showed her a letter that convinced her.''

"Did you see the letter?'' Smith asked, leaning forward.

Jake answered him. "No, neither of us did. Mom said she recognized the handwriting and knew it was authentic. But she said it had some personal things in it that neither she nor Connor wanted revealed.''

"And you didn't demand to see it?'' Smith asked, surprise in his voice.

"Obviously you don't know Megan Maitland well,'' Michael said dryly. "She's a strong woman.''

A tap on the study door distracted them. The butler's voice came through the wood. "Dinner is served.''

"We'd better go or Mom will be back to check on us,'' Jake assured them all, standing and pulling Camille to her feet.

"Before we go," Smith said, "can you recommend a good private investigation firm?"

"Why?" Jake asked, his brows lowering.

"I want to hire someone to get to the bottom of all these strange events and give me back my identity."

CHAPTER FIVE

JAKE DIVIDED his attention between Camille and the first Connor, who sat at Megan's right. Jake had to admit Camille's observation had been on the mark. The first Connor wasn't a man he would ever enjoy having as a cousin.

He remembered thinking of his mother when Smith—Connor?—had raised his eyebrow in challenge. Jake could see nothing in the first Connor that reminded him of his classy mother. Of course, Connor was adopted, and Megan was a Maitland only by marriage, so there shouldn't have been any shared traits.

After-dinner coffee was served in the large salon where they'd had the hors d'oeuvres. Jake noted the first Connor stuck to Megan's side like glue.

Jake quickly grew tired of exercising his social skills. They were kind of rusty, anyway, and he was anxious to get Camille safely home. But he hated to cut short her first social outing in months. She seemed to be enjoying herself, visiting with his two older sisters, Abby and Anna.

He drew closer, noting Camille's animation. It hadn't occurred to him that she might be missing female companionship.

He moved to her side.

"Jake, doesn't Camille's dress look fabulous?" Anna asked, beaming at him, obviously proud of her efforts.

"Yeah, she looks great," he said, avoiding Camille's gaze. "You did a terrific job, Anna." He leaned over and kissed her on the cheek. He wasn't usually demonstrative, so both his sisters stared at him in shock.

"Hey, I delivered the baby!" Abby said. "Don't I get a kiss?"

"Sure," he agreed, complying.

As he stepped back from Abby, Anna said, "But Camille's the one who did most of the work. She shouldn't be left out." The twinkle in her eyes told Jake she knew he'd be bothered by her suggestion.

As the youngest son, he'd always tried to prove himself to his older siblings. That competitive spirit surged through him now, and he leaned over to kiss Camille's cheek as he had his sisters', striving to keep his cool.

But his reaction to kissing Camille was immediate. The flame of desire that had been lit when he'd helped with her disguise flared brightly.

"What's this?" Michael asked, stepping forward with a grin. "A kissing fest with Jake?"

Jake ignored the teasing and turned the subject to local politics.

Several minutes later, Camille touched his arm. "Jake, are we staying much longer? I'm very tired."

She immediately had his full attention. "Are you all right?"

"Yes, of course," she said, giving him one of those

warm smiles he'd come to crave. "But I thought I'd go upstairs and feed Jamie before we start home. Shall I go now?"

"Yeah," he said with relief. At last he could escape.

"What about the disguise? Should I put it on again?"

Jake shook his head. Just her question made him think of those treacherous moments when he'd touched her. He cleared his throat. "I think you'll be okay without the disguise. It's dark outside."

With a nod, she slipped from the room.

After watching her until he could no longer see her, he turned to find Michael staring at him. "What?" he asked with a frown.

"You couldn't take your eyes off her. I thought you said it was business."

"It is!" Jake snapped. "It is. I'm her bodyguard, remember? I'm supposed to keep an eye on her."

"Uh-huh," Michael said with a big grin.

Damn. He was going to have to watch himself. "I've got to find Garrett and Max."

"They're talking across the room. Are you going to tell them about what we found out?"

Jake frowned and put a finger to his lips. "No. We don't say anything until we know."

"I'm worried about protecting your mother."

"She'll be all right." He hoped. He didn't want his mother at risk, but as long as the first Connor didn't suspect anything was wrong, Jake figured they had some time.

Assuming this new Connor wasn't lying.

He said good-night to Michael and crossed the large room. Garrett and Max greeted him.

"Are you two about ready to head out? Camille is feeding Jamie. Then she'll be ready to leave."

Max grinned. "Hell, I was ready to leave as soon as we ate. I can't take much more of your cousin Connor. Hard to believe you're related."

"I know. He's not my favorite relation, either. But Mom is thrilled."

"Your mother has a big heart," Garrett said, his gaze on Megan and Connor across the room. "By the way, that TV woman Chelsea Markum got word of the party. She tried to get in a few minutes before dinner. She didn't see Camille, did she? We couldn't find either one of you."

"We were in the study with Harrison Smith, chatting."

Garrett raised an eyebrow. "Anything interesting?"

"A tidbit or two that might pay off. We'll see." He rubbed his forehead. "Why would Chelsea come here? This is a family party."

Max frowned, too. "The woman will go to any lengths to scoop out a story. I think she pays someone at the caterers to keep her informed."

"If Chatty Cathy broadcasts anything about the party, there's a good chance Eckart will hear. Let's be extra careful."

"Right," Max agreed. "That woman is enough to drive a man crazy."

Jake heard a personal note in his friend's voice. Surely Max wasn't attracted to the nosy reporter?

Camille entered the room, her child in her arms. The women in his family rushed to her side to see the baby. Jake frowned. He didn't think it would be good to expose Jamie to all those germs.

He hurried to Camille's side. "She'll show off her baby another time," he said, slipping between his sisters and sisters-in-law to rescue Camille and Jamie. "We have to go now."

He escorted Camille to his mother so she could say her goodbyes, then to the front hall, where Garrett and Max stood waiting.

"I've asked for our vehicles," Garrett told him, opening the front door as the glare of approaching headlights alerted them to the car's arrival.

Jake took Camille's arm and started toward the door.

The butler called as Garrett headed outside. "Mr. Lord! There's a phone call."

"Take a number," Jake ordered. He was anxious to get out of there.

"I'd better take it, Jake," Garrett said, a frown on his face. He hurried into the butler's pantry.

Jake shifted his weight from one foot to the other. "Need me to take the baby?"

Camille gave him a tired smile that touched him. "That would be nice, if you don't mind."

They made the transfer, and he realized Jamie was awake. "Isn't it past his bedtime?"

"His bedtime is kind of flexible," Camille reminded him.

Max moved closer. "Hey, I think he's grown since I last saw him."

With motherly pride, Camille said, "Well, he is a week older. And he's a hearty eater."

Jake couldn't help it. His gaze immediately focused on Camille's breasts, outlined beneath the shimmery green material. He hoped there weren't any other social occasions when she'd be wearing that dress. It distracted him too easily.

"Jake!" Garrett called, motioning from the doorway. "Max, you, too. We've got a problem."

CAMILLE GRABBED the baby carrier as Jake turned to see what Garrett needed. With a muttered apology, he released the carrier and left her standing alone in the open entryway. Then he turned around, locked the front door and led her to a chair farther from the foyer. "Stay here."

She drew a deep breath and pulled the carrier closer to her. Jamie stirred, trying to stretch. "Easy, little one. Jake will be back in a minute, and we'll go home." She hoped. Garrett had sounded ominous.

She kept her gaze focused on the door to the butler's pantry, but she couldn't see anyone.

Suddenly Jake's voice cut through the silence. "You've got ten minutes or your ass is in a sling." The angry words were followed by the noise of the receiver being slammed down.

Jake walked out of the pantry and immediately to Camille, his eyes full of anger.

"What's wrong?"

"Nothing to worry about," he said with a tight smile.

"Jake, I need to know. Don't lie to me."

He squatted in front of her and covered one of her hands holding the baby carrier. "There's a car parked on the road with its lights out. A man is sitting behind the wheel, waiting."

She gasped, then slowly drew a deep breath to calm herself. "You think it's Vince?"

"I don't know, but there's no point in taking chances."

With a coolness that belied her fluttering heart, she asked, "What are we going to do?"

"The FBI team will be here to check him out in a few minutes."

Unexpectedly, she laughed. "Would that be in *ten* minutes?"

"You heard, huh?" he asked with a grin. "I guess I lost my temper. The idiot assured me it was probably nothing."

Camille frowned. "He doesn't sound very interested in his work."

"No, he doesn't. Thanks for not going hysterical on me."

Her eyebrows arched, and she glared at him. "When have I ever gotten hysterical?"

"Never," he assured her. "But most women would have by now. You're stronger than you look."

She forgave him at once. "Just promise to keep Jamie safe," she said.

He stood and reached down to cup her cheek. "I'll keep both of you safe, I promise."

She covered his hand with her own, holding it against her skin, loving his touch, his scent.

He bent toward her, as if he intended to kiss her,

and she forgot to breathe. Then Garrett called his name.

"Max and I are going to drive around the block."

"I'll go with you," Jake replied. "Just let me get Michael to keep an eye on Camille."

"No!" Camille exclaimed, grasping Jake's suit coat to keep him from moving. "Vince would recognize you. He might—it could be dangerous."

"She's got a point," Max said as he and Garrett moved closer. "You'd better let the FBI team handle everything."

"Then why are you two going out there?" Jake demanded.

"We need to know when to leave. We can't see anything from inside the gates," Garrett explained.

She could tell Jake didn't like being left behind, but he finally nodded. "Okay, but don't take any chances."

The two men nodded and hurried out the front door.

Camille leaned back in her chair and gave a sigh of relief. "How will they let us know?"

"Garrett has a car phone. He'll call here." Jake moved to the front porch, nodding at the butler, who was standing at attention in the entryway.

Even as she opened her mouth to protest, Jake stepped to the side, out of the lights. He knew what he was doing, she reminded herself. But she couldn't help worrying.

The distant sound of sirens surprised her. She was sure the FBI didn't use sirens. Maybe there was another emergency nearby.

Jake came racing inside and headed for the phone in the butler's pantry. She couldn't distinguish his words, but she could recognize his fury. Again the phone was slammed down. A few seconds later she heard his voice once more.

Picking up the baby carrier, she crossed to the door of the pantry. "Jake?"

He held up a finger in warning. "Yes, sir, I guess you could call it a mistake in judgment, but I can think of a few other words. I want someone down here who intends to do the job. Not someone who's worried about getting his beauty sleep!" He listened intently. "Yes, sir, thank you." Then he hung up the phone.

"What happened?"

"I'll explain in the car. Let's go." He took the baby carrier in one hand and her arm in the other and started outside just as Garrett and Max drove up.

Max jumped out. "We'd better go. The cops are chasing the car."

"We're ready," Jake said as he opened the back door and strapped Jamie in. Then he opened the passenger door for Camille. Before she realized his intent, he grasped her waist and swung her into the front seat. "Get your seat belt on."

As if she didn't know to do that? She had it fastened before he slid behind the wheel. Max, in the meantime, had gotten in his pickup behind them, and Garrett started down the drive in his car.

"Duck down," Jake ordered.

Reluctantly, Camille did as she was told, even though she didn't like it. She wanted to see what was happening. But she'd promised to do exactly as Jake ordered when he'd finally agreed to be her protector.

"What's going on?" she asked, her voice muffled because her face was pressed against her knees.

"Nothing."

A most unsatisfactory answer. "Then can I—"

"No!"

"But, Jake—"

The phone rang.

"Yeah?" Jake said as he answered, his voice tight with tension. "You're sure?"

Camille's heartbeat sped up.

"Damn! Okay, we'll handle it that way. Tell Garrett." Jake hung up. "You're going to have to stay down a little longer. We've picked up a tail."

"But I thought the cops were chasing—"

"Either a mistake…or a decoy. Since whoever is chasing us hasn't seen you, we're going to go in three different directions and meet up later. With any luck he'll choose one of the others to follow."

"And if he doesn't?" She hated the fear in her voice, but she was scared.

"Then we'll outrun him. I know Austin, and he doesn't. I'll lose him."

A thought suddenly occurred to her. "He can't see the baby seat, can he?"

Jake looked over his shoulder. "Nope, it's below window level. Since Jamie's so little, he's out of sight. When he gets bigger, we'll—" He caught himself and stopped. "I mean, I'm sure this will be resolved before he gets bigger."

She prayed he was right.

"Hold on," Jake warned, and made a sharp turn to the right.

Camille did as he said. Then she turned her face so her cheek rested on her knees and she could watch Jake. Keeping him in sight gave her confidence they would make it safely home.

After all, Jake was her protector.

JAKE couldn't believe what was happening. He'd known there was a risk in bringing Camille to the party, but he hadn't wanted to disappoint his mother. And he'd taken precautions.

But Steve Parks's response had upset him. Steve was Jake's FBI contact in Austin, and Jake had expected more from him. He'd figured the leak to Eckart was coming from D.C. Now he wasn't so sure. But if it was Steve, it wouldn't be for much longer. Jake's boss had promised a replacement at once. Calling the cops so he wouldn't have to get out of bed had been a big mistake. And Jake intended to see that Steve paid for it.

"Are we being followed?"

He glanced at Camille's sweet face, then trained his gaze on the road again. "Can't tell yet. There's still a lot of traffic."

"Can you tell me what happened?"

"Steve called the cops to do his job. He didn't want to get out of bed." He appreciated Camille's gasp. She, at least, understood the lapse in judgment. Too bad Steve hadn't.

"And they came with their sirens on? Wouldn't it have made more sense to sneak up on him?"

"You've got a good head, Camille. Want to go to work for the Company when this is over?" He grinned but kept his gaze alternating between the road and the rearview mirror.

"I don't think so. I'd like to have a normal life again."

Her words distracted him. Since he'd returned to Texas with Camille, he'd had those same thoughts. A life like his siblings had, without all the recent drama of abandoned babies and long-lost relations popping up, of course.

The phone rang. Jake grabbed it. "Yeah, Max. He is? Okay. I'm going left on Sixth."

He made the turn just as the light turned yellow. Traffic was heavier on the popular street, so he couldn't go as fast, but he watched in the rearview mirror as a dark sedan almost caused a wreck turning on to Sixth.

"There he is."

"Is it Vince?"

"He's too far away for me to be sure. Max was following him, but he got caught at the light."

"How did he know to follow us?"

"Because the car in the middle always carries the important people."

"Oh."

Jake took a sharp right and pressed on the accelerator. Then he made another left, his tires squealing.

After several more maneuvers, Camille prayed she wouldn't throw up. That would only add to her misery, but all these turns with her head down were making her queasy.

The phone rang again.

"Yeah," Jake answered. "I'm going west on Lamar, getting ready to take Thirty-eighth over to Mo-Pac."

He listened for several seconds, then asked, "Where's Garrett?"

Camille watched his face. She knew if either of the men was in danger, she'd see concern on his face. But he showed no panic as he said, "All right. We'll meet there."

He hung up and glanced at her. "Max is behind us again. We're meeting Garrett on the outskirts of town."

"Have we lost the guy following us yet?"

He shook his head. "I don't think so. He's pretty determined."

If the man was Vince, she already knew that. After all, he'd been after her for six months.

"Damn!" Jake exclaimed, and sped up. "He's back on our tail."

"Hurry, Jake!" Camille urged.

Then a bullet pierced the back window of the SUV.

CHAPTER SIX

CAMILLE SCREAMED and started to sit up, but Jake shoved her down. "Stay down!"

"But Jamie!" she cried, trying to elude his hold.

Jake looked over his shoulder. "Jamie's fine. The window didn't shatter, and the bullet was too high to hit him. Even if the glass had shattered, I don't think it would come over the back seat."

They heard several other bullets, and Jake ducked without thinking, but they never felt the bullets strike the SUV. He looked in the mirror. "I think that was Max shooting. The sedan has pulled over with a flat tire."

"Do you want to go back?" she asked quietly.

Jake jerked his gaze to her. "No! I won't put you and Jamie in danger, no matter what."

"But if you caught him, it would all be over."

Jake ignored her and picked up the phone. "Garrett? Max shot out one of the guy's tires. I think he may have gone back to have a look." He gave Garrett their location, then hung up.

"Garrett is only a couple of minutes away. He'll be there to help Max before you know it. And we're heading for the ranch."

"Can I sit up now?"

"Yeah."

She released her seat belt before he knew what she was doing and got on her knees to check on Jamie.

"He's sleeping," she said, almost with a sob.

"Good. Get your seat belt back on. I don't want you in danger."

She did as he said, sitting with her hands clasped tightly together.

Before they reached the ranch, the phone rang again. Jake grabbed the receiver, hoping all was well.

"Jake, he got away," Max said, regret in his voice. "I chased him on foot, but he's damned fast. I lost him."

"Thanks for trying. Get the license plate number."

"I already did, but it's a rental."

"We can still check to see who rented it. If nothing else, we might find an alias he's using."

"Right, first thing in the morning. I'm coming out to the ranch to spend the night. Thought I might try a little camping," Max added.

"Let me know when you're in place," Jake said before he hung up.

"Is everything okay?" Camille immediately asked.

"Yeah, but he got away."

"What did you mean about someone being in place?"

"Max is coming out to the ranch. He'll set up watch outside."

Camille frowned. "But he won't get much sleep."

Jake chuckled. "Yeah, and frankly, I'm glad. If I were having to rely on Steve, we'd be in big trouble."

"But the man wasn't able to follow us. So we'll be safe?"

He heard a slight wobble in her voice and reached out his hand to cover both of hers. "Of course we'll be fine. Max is just erring on the side of caution."

Neither spoke again until Jake turned off the main highway. When he shut off the headlights, Camille gasped.

"Why did you do that?"

"There was no one behind us when I turned off, but I don't want anyone to notice us from the highway. There's a full moon. I can see well enough."

Again silence reigned until he pulled his vehicle to a stop behind the little cabin they called home. When Camille reached for the door handle, he stopped her. "Wait."

"What? Is something wrong?"

"I want you to stay in the car with the doors locked while I check things out."

"You think someone's here?" she asked with a gasp, one hand going to her throat.

"No, I don't. But, like Max, we're going to err on the side of caution. If I'm not back out here in five minutes, you slide behind the wheel and drive to the city. And call the police."

"Jake—be careful," she said softly, reaching out to touch his arm.

He carried her hand to his lips. "Count on it." And he got out, waiting to make sure she locked the door behind him. Then he strode to the back door of the cabin.

AFTER CHECKING again on Jamie, Camille stared at the cabin. They'd left the kitchen light on, but the rest of the rooms were dark. She could trace Jake's progress as he walked through the cabin, turning on lights.

She wished she could as easily trace her emotions. She loved Jake Maitland. She knew he'd become important to her. He'd been her constant companion since Christmas.

But tonight, socializing with others, she'd realized just how much the man meant to her. He was the center of her world in a crowd as much as he was when they were alone. All other men paled beside him in her eyes. And when his life, as well as hers and her child's, had been threatened, she thought she'd die.

Now he was putting his life at risk—again—to protect her and Jamie.

But life wouldn't be worth living if he died.

She would have to let him go, of course. Being out with him tonight might have made her realize how much he meant to her, but it had also told her that she didn't belong in his world of wealth and power. She was definitely middle-class.

When he appeared in the doorway and walked to the car, she breathed a sigh of relief and unlocked the door. "Everything's all right?"

"Yeah." He opened the back door and unstrapped Jamie's carrier. Then he led the way into the cabin.

Camille took the carrier from Jake. "I'll put Jamie to bed." She expected Jake to disappear to his room.

He never lingered when they reached home. Tonight, however, he followed her into the baby's room.

Camille lifted Jamie out of the carrier and, in spite of his being asleep, held him tightly against her. She needed to feel her tiny son's heart beating, to have the comfort of his warmth against her.

To her surprise, Jake reached out and gently rubbed his hand over Jamie's head. "He was a good soldier."

Camille's chuckle was frayed around the edges, but at least she wasn't crying. "He didn't know what was going on. And I don't want him to be a soldier."

"What do you want him to be?" Jake whispered.

"Happy," she said at once. "Maybe he'll be a doctor, or a cowboy, or—I don't know, a banker. As long as he's happy."

"He will be. With you for a mother, he'll have a great life."

His words were sweet, but they were too much for her. Still holding Jamie snugly against her, she turned and buried her face in Jake's chest. "I almost got him killed," she said with a sob.

His arms cradled her against him. "No, sweetheart, you protected him. Eckart is the one who endangered his own son's life. But Jamie's safe now."

She wanted to stay there in his arms. But she knew she was taking advantage of his gallantry. She kissed his cheek. "Thanks to you." Then she backed away and turned to put Jamie in his bed.

Her son stirred and stretched, his eyes still closed, before settling beneath his blanket.

"He can sleep through anything," Jake whispered, reaching out to pat the baby's stomach.

"Thank goodness."

Still conscious of his warmth near her, she backed away from the bed.

Jake turned to look at her. "You'd better settle down, too. You've had a long night."

"Yes. I'm definitely ready to get out of this dress. It's lovely, but not very comfortable."

She hurried toward the connecting door to her room.

"Uh, Camille?"

"Yes?"

"I don't think I told you how—how beautiful you looked tonight. And how brave you were."

Jake's words had a powerful effect on her. Although he'd kept his distance these past months, he'd still tried to meet her every need. He'd been more successful than he would ever know. It was a good thing he wasn't aware of what she really wanted from him.

Finally, she smiled. "Thanks, Jake."

Then she closed the door behind her, leaning against it, her heart pounding even harder than it had when Vince had fired at them.

JAKE STARED at the little boy sleeping in his baby bed. The man had actually shot at them tonight, knowing his son was in the car. Not to mention Camille. How could he?

If Jamie were his son, he'd— He stopped himself. He'd best not think that way. But Jamie was special. And his mother even more so. Not only was she a wonderful mother, she was also courageous and patient.

The baby stirred again, making a small noise, his fist finding its way to his cupid's bow mouth. "Hey, little guy, you can't be hungry yet," Jake whispered. "Your mom fed you not too long ago." He stopped to look at his watch. Well, it'd been over two hours ago.

With a frown he moved into the hallway and stopped outside Camille's room. Leaning his head against the door, he listened, trying to determine if she'd gone to sleep.

At first he heard nothing. Then he recognized the sound of sobs. Though muffled, they were definitely sobs. He opened the door without knocking and discovered a miserable Camille curled into a sodden ball on the bed.

Her elegant gown was strewn across the end of the bed. He was grateful she'd put on a cotton robe before she'd given in to her misery.

"Honey, don't cry," Jake said as he made his way toward her and gathered her into his arms. "Everything's going to be all right."

She didn't answer other than to shake her head.

Jake pushed a pillow behind his back and settled against it on the bed, still holding her.

"Camille, I promised I'd protect you. You and Jamie. We're getting near the end. Soon this will all be over." While he softly talked, he stroked her warm body, trying to calm her. Unfortunately, it had the opposite effect on him.

The more he touched her, the more he realized how

much he'd come to admire her, to want her. He'd always found her courageous, but she was so much more. And there was an inexplicable chemistry between them.

The first time he'd touched her, in support, before they'd gone into hiding, a surge of hunger had filled him, so he'd made sure he kept his distance. But when she went into labor, he hadn't been able to hold back. And after putting her disguise on her tonight, he had little resistance left.

His hands stilled on her back as he cuddled her against him. What was he doing? Testing his discipline? Not a good idea.

But he couldn't abandon her now.

He lowered his voice and crooned to her as he would a child. Making his strokes soothing and languorous, he breathed deeply to slow his rapid pulse. But with her warm body pressed against his and her breasts resting on his chest, it wasn't an easy task.

He closed his eyes and tried to think of something boring while he held Camille. Eventually, he began softly singing a lullaby his mother had used to calm him when he'd had a nightmare.

It had a soothing effect on Camille…and him, reminding him of his childhood, surrounded by family, safe and secure.

FIRST the phone rang.

Then Jamie wailed.

Jake and Camille came awake at the same time.

She almost leaped straight off the bed. "What— what's going on?"

Jake didn't move quite as fast. "I was, uh, comforting you and—and I guess we fell asleep." He cleared his throat. "Get the baby. I'll get the phone."

He sprinted for the kitchen.

"Jake, did I wake you?" Max asked, sounding puzzled. "I thought you'd be waiting to hear from me."

"Yeah, but Jamie just woke up. We were tending to him." The kid wouldn't mind being used as an excuse. He checked his watch. "What took so long?"

"A cop came along. He insisted on hearing the whole story. He checked my permit and everything."

"Sorry, pal. Look, I think everything is okay here. Why don't you go to the ranch house and beg Garrett for a bed and get some rest?"

"Nah, I've got a sleeping bag from him. I'm going to sleep in the back of my pickup. I've even got an air mattress. I'll be fine. Can I join you for coffee in the morning?"

"Of course."

"Good. I'll see you around eight."

Since it was almost three, Jake knew Max would need that coffee. He would, too. He just hoped Camille was speaking to him in the morning. She'd been a little upset when they'd awakened.

He tiptoed to her room. The door was still open. He peeked around it to discover Camille in the rocker, nursing her baby. "How's he doing? Any nightmares?"

"No. Jake, I'm sorry about earlier."

"There's nothing to be sorry for. I'm the one who fell asleep."

"I fell asleep, too," she assured him, her gaze anxious.

He crossed to her side and leaned down to kiss her brow. Touching her was becoming a habit. "So it's no one's fault."

"But I was crying!"

Jamie started to fuss at his mother's raised voice, so Camille had to reposition him.

Jake squatted beside the rocker. "Do you know, that's the first time in six months that you've cried? I find that pretty amazing."

Her cheeks bloomed, and she looked away. "That's the first time you've caught me."

He chuckled. "I'll have to be more vigilant in the future."

"I'm no longer pregnant. I'll do better."

"Don't get too much better, because you're just about perfect right now. I wouldn't be good enough to wipe your shoes if you get better."

"You're being silly."

Jake stood. "I'm going to set the timer on the coffeepot and prepare it for the morning. I'll check on you in a minute."

When he reached the kitchen, he leaned against the cabinet and inhaled deeply. He'd been faking calm since he'd awakened with Camille in his arms.

She'd felt so right, snuggled against him, encircling him with her scent, her warmth. He'd never wanted to let her go.

But he had to. He had no right to claim her. Besides, he had no intention of marrying, let alone having children. Could he be a good father? He and his own father hadn't had the best of relationships.

Well, that wasn't quite true. It was when he'd hit the teen years that they'd disagreed. But that didn't matter. What mattered now was Camille, and the lascivious thoughts he was having of her. Of the ways he wanted to touch her. Of how much he wanted her.

He had to stop all that. He certainly couldn't pursue her romantically when her safety depended on him. Besides, she wasn't the type for a fling.

But when this whole situation with Vince was over? Would she and Jamie just disappear from his life? Camille was a homebody. Jake was an FBI agent. The direction of their lives couldn't be further apart. He needed to regain the distance he'd kept before Jamie arrived.

He groaned. Now that he'd held her, touched her, could he do that? He thought back to the night Jamie was born. When the nurse had placed the baby in his arms to hand to Camille, as if he were the husband, the father, he'd felt an attachment he'd been fighting ever since. He wasn't winning the battle.

What if— His breath caught. What if he had something more permanent in mind? When Vincent Eckart was captured, could he and Camille explore the feelings he'd been suppressing for so long? Or would she flee from all memory of the nightmare they'd shared?

And could he really think of settling down—like his siblings? Staying in one place? Committing to a future of fatherhood?

He didn't know.

JAKE DIDN'T RETURN.

Camille wasn't surprised, after she'd taken advantage of him the way she had. He'd never led her on. Every time she'd reached out to him and he'd responded, he'd quietly made it clear that he was only doing his job.

Even in the delivery room.

He definitely was an expert at doing his job, though.

She guessed that would be his explanation for holding her tonight as she'd sobbed. Her well-being was his responsibility—both physical and emotional.

Even touching her. When his lips had touched her brow so lovingly, she'd wanted to kiss him back, to pull him closer.

Guilt filled her. But tonight she'd needed his warmth, his protection, his strength.

She'd believed, mistakenly, that Vince wanted her and the baby alive. That even if he kidnapped her and Jamie, he wouldn't hurt them. Maybe a few slaps, but he wouldn't kill them.

Tonight she'd been proven wrong. He'd fired at them knowing she and Jamie were in the vehicle. Even if he'd been aiming at Jake, a crash could have killed them.

And the enormity of that realization had overwhelmed her.

Okay, good excuse for taking advantage of Jake, but you've got to be stronger. You can't make his job so difficult. After all, he was male, and definitely human. But he'd made it clear he didn't want her. He was the good guy, the one in the white hat. She'd been married to the black-hatted villain.

She burped her son, then tiptoed to the nursery and tucked Jamie in his bed. He looked so sweet, so peaceful, lying there under his blue blanket. He had no idea what a difficult place his world could be.

She kissed him good-night and hurried to her room. Before she got ready for bed, she hung up the dress she'd worn. It was an exquisite gown, and she gave thanks that Anna had known what she should wear. She'd felt as well dressed as the other women.

She sighed, pausing at the closet door. But clothes couldn't change the person she was. She wasn't a Maitland or a peer of the Maitlands. She didn't fit in.

She was a gangster's ex. Of course, she hadn't known Vince's criminal connections when she'd married him. Jake had doubted that fact in the beginning, but she thought he believed her now.

Vince had told her he sold insurance. But she felt her reputation was stained by her association with him. She was ashamed of her naiveté. It would haunt her the rest of her life.

The Maitland women wouldn't ordinarily have welcomed her into their midst. It was Jake they'd wanted to see, and it was only out of duty that he'd escorted her to his mother's party tonight.

She'd best remember those truths. Lying in Jake's arms might be heaven for her, but it was an impossible heaven, one she needed to forget.

After changing into her pajamas, she turned off the light and slipped into bed. The pillow still held Jake's scent, and she breathed deeply of his expensive cologne, his male essence.

She might not be able to have Jake Maitland in her life, but she could dream of him, as she surely would tonight. No one could take away her dreams.

As she lay there in the darkness, she heard her door inch open. Any other time, she would've sprung up, sure Vince had discovered her hiding place.

But she knew, without looking, that Jake was checking on her. If she let him know she was awake, they'd have to have another awkward discussion, and she'd have to apologize for letting him hold her.

She couldn't force that lie to come out tonight. Instead, if she faced him now, she'd plead with him to hold her the rest of the night. She'd beg him to give her his strength. She'd reach out and touch him.

Camille lay perfectly still, breathing evenly, until she heard the door close and quiet footsteps head toward the kitchen.

She was alone.

Her future held more of the same—if she had a future—so she'd better get used to it.

CHAPTER SEVEN

WHEN JAKE HEARD Jamie four hours later, he rolled out of bed, rubbing the grit from his eyes. It wasn't the first time he'd gone short of sleep, and it wouldn't be the last.

He hurried to the kitchen and prepared scrambled eggs and buttered toast. He put them on a tray, added a glass of milk and carried the breakfast down the hall to Camille's room.

"Come in," she called softly in response to his knock.

"How's he doing?" he asked, staring at the two of them, thinking again of Madonna and child. How could two people so sweet and pure be connected to Vincent Eckart?

"Fine. I'm sorry he woke you."

Jake grinned. "Don't apologize. I needed to be up, but I didn't bother to set an alarm clock. Jamie is as good as any rooster."

Camille pretended outrage. "You're comparing my sweet baby to a rooster?"

"You're right," Jake said with a chuckle. He loved her sense of the ridiculous. "A rooster can't compare to Jamie's screams."

She rolled her eyes and laughed. "You have a point."

"Is he about finished? I fixed you some breakfast. I thought you could eat and go back to sleep. Make up for our late night." His gaze fell to the child in her arms. Then he hurriedly looked away, hoping she hadn't noticed that Jamie had fallen asleep, his mouth near but not covering the rosebud nipple of her breast. "I'll put the tray over here," he said, moving to the other side of the bed, behind the rocker.

He could tell she'd discovered her naked breast by the scarlet in her cheeks, but he pretended he didn't see her embarrassment. If only he could erase the sight from his memory.

"Thank you, but I'm not really hungry." As she spoke, she moved the baby to her shoulder to burp him.

"Uh-uh, I'm the burping detail. You have to eat to have enough milk for junior here. That's your duty." He reached out for the warm little body and snuggled Jamie against his shoulder. "Hey, he's wiggling a lot this morning."

Camille, her robe properly fastened, crossed to the bed and sat by the tray. "Jake, you shouldn't have brought me breakfast in bed. I mean, breakfast to my room!"

"New moms need a break," he said, ignoring her panic. "Especially after last night. I was exhausted when we left the party. Then we had our little adventure. It's no wonder we both fell asleep last night."

He watched her carefully to see how she would react to mention of their little nap a few hours ago.

She took a small bite of scrambled egg and chewed it slowly. Finally she said, ''I'm sorry I caused you so much trouble last night.''

''You didn't—''

Jamie let out a loud burp, interrupting his protest. Then he heard Max knocking on the back door. ''Max is here.''

Camille stood and came to his side. ''I'll put Jamie to bed.''

''Thanks. Then go back to sleep, okay?''

She gave him an exasperated look, her brows high. ''You know, for someone who doesn't want to be connected to his family's clinic, you sure do hand out a lot of medical advice, Dr. Jake.''

''Damn straight,'' he assured her. ''And if you don't follow it, I'll give you bad-tasting medicine.''

She made a face at him and walked into Jamie's room.

Jake reluctantly hurried to the kitchen to open the back door.

''Did I wake you?'' Max asked as he entered.

''Hell, no, not with alarm-clock Jamie in the building.''

Max grinned. ''Yeah, I've heard new babies don't sleep much.''

''Oh, he sleeps a lot, but only in short stretches. He's up every four hours, rain or shine.'' While he talked, Jake grabbed a couple of mugs and filled them with coffee before joining Max at the table. After taking a sip, he rubbed his face with both hands. ''You want something to eat? I can—''

''Garrett is bringing breakfast.''

"That's neighborly," Jake said with a grin. "I gather you've talked with him this morning?"

"Yeah, he was *my* alarm clock."

The sound of a motor approaching had Jake moving to the kitchen window. Once he'd identified Garrett's SUV, he grabbed another mug and poured more coffee.

Jake swung open the door to Garrett, who moved inside carrying two large dishes. "I hope you've got coffee ready."

"Your housekeeper didn't fix you any?"

"Of course she did. But one cup isn't going to be enough this morning." He set the plates down and saw the extra mug of coffee. Grabbing it, he took a sip. "Mmm, I think I'm going to live."

Jake grinned. These guys should try all-night stake-outs for six days in a row. *Then* they'd realize what it was like to be sleep-deprived. Now that he thought of it, he realized he didn't want to go through that kind of misery ever again.

"Bacon and eggs and cinnamon rolls," Garrett said, waving toward the covered dishes.

Max didn't wait for a second invitation. Jake grabbed three plates and forks, and the men spent the next few minutes filling their stomachs.

Jake stopped eating suddenly. "I should take a cinnamon roll to Camille. She needs to put on some weight." He leaped to his feet, got a saucer and slid a cinnamon roll onto it. "I'll be back in a minute."

Garrett and Max exchanged a look when Jake left the room. "Does he know he's gone over the edge?" Garrett asked.

Max shook his head. "Nope, he's just doing his duty...according to Jake. Nothing personal."

"Personal, hell. Last night—" He broke off as Jake came into the kitchen, still carrying the cinnamon roll.

"She's asleep. I'll warm it up for her later." He covered the roll with a napkin. "I'm not putting it back on the plate because one of you mangy critters might eat it."

"Hey! You were as fast to the trough as I was," Max protested.

Jake grinned. "I know."

They finished off the rest of the breakfast in companionable silence.

"Now, I thought we ought to have a powwow this morning and take stock," Garrett said at last. "It seems to me things are heating up."

"In more ways than one," Jake muttered.

"What do you mean? Are you talking about you and Camille?" Garrett asked.

Jake turned a bright red. "No! I don't know what *you're* talking about!"

"Then what are you talking about?" Garrett asked in a reasonable tone of voice.

Jake immediately sacrificed the appearance of the second Connor to distract Garrett from any questions about his relationship with Camille. Besides, he didn't have any answers where that was concerned.

"We have two Connors." His statement grabbed the other men's attention. He quickly explained about Harrison Smith's surprising revelation last night, then waited for their reaction.

"This is a relief, actually," Garrett said after considering his words.

"How do you figure that?" Jake asked.

"I never liked Connor. The first Connor. And I felt guilty about it. Your mom is the most wonderful person in the world. I didn't want her to be disappointed, but I knew the man—" He broke off, as if reluctant to say any more.

Max didn't have that difficulty. "Has no class, unlike Jake's mother."

All three men nodded in agreement.

"You're right," Jake agreed. "I was blaming my aunt and uncle for raising him so badly, and I never met them."

"Smith, on the other hand," Garrett said, his gaze narrowed, as if picturing the man, "seems to have a lot of class." He looked at Jake. "So what are we going to do?"

"The man agreed that it would be best to keep Mom in the dark for the moment."

Garrett nodded. Then he asked, "What about the baby?"

Max straightened. "Hey, yeah, is Chase really a Maitland? Or part of a scam?"

Jake shrugged. "Smith says he had nothing to do with Janelle, even though she was his mother's maid. Obviously, someone's lying in this whole mess, but I'm not sure who yet." He paused and then added, "There's another curious twist to this story that involves Sara, Shelby's chef at Austin Eats."

"The one with amnesia!" Max exclaimed, his eyes widening. "What about her?"

"It seems she used to work for Smith at the same time that Janelle did."

Garrett scratched his head. "That's a strange co-incidence...unless she's part of whatever's going on with Janelle and the first Connor."

"Yeah," Jake agreed with a sigh.

"And on top of that, we've got Eckart running around loose," Max said. "Sorry we couldn't catch him last night, Jake."

"Hey, you tried. If Steve Parks hadn't been so un-cooperative, we might've wrapped things up then. Instead, we put Camille and the baby in danger."

"No, it's not your fault," a soft voice said from the doorway.

Jake spun around, surprised to see Camille standing there. She was dressed in some of her new clothes, trim walking shorts with a matching knit top. She looked good. Damn good. He swallowed. "I thought you were asleep."

The other two men stood, and Jake leaped to his feet.

"I heard you check on me. I thought maybe you needed something." She was carrying the tray he'd brought to her earlier, and she crossed to the sink to empty it. "Are you having a private conference? Do I need to disappear?"

"No!" Jake exclaimed. He moved to the counter near her, and handed her the saucer with the cinnamon roll on it. "Sit down and eat this. I'll get you some more milk."

"I'm not hungry. You fixed me a big breakfast."

"And you didn't eat even half of it. You're going to dry up and blow away if you don't eat."

"Jake, really—"

"You two sound like an old married couple," Max said with a big grin on his face. "You'd better eat the damn roll, Camille, or Mother Jake here will hound you all day."

Jake glared at Max, but the man accomplished what Jake had been unable to do. Camille took the saucer and sat down at the table.

"Fine, but no milk. Ice water will be better."

Jake put a glass of water in front of her and resumed his seat, but he kept his gaze on her. She closed her eyes after taking the first bite, then licked the sugary icing off her finger.

Jake's mouth watered. He wanted to taste her skin, to…he jerked his gaze away, and it collided with the grins on his friends' faces. "What?"

"Nothing," Garrett assured him. "Does Camille know about, uh, what we were talking about?"

"Yeah, she was there."

"The two Connors?" she asked.

"Yeah. She helped me and Michael question the man."

Max leaned forward. "This second Connor kind of changes things, doesn't he?"

"Yeah," Garrett agreed. "Megan's been waiting for Janelle to get hold of Chase's birth certificate. Now, with two Connors, how will we know which one is really the father?"

"Janelle doesn't have the birth certificate with her?" Camille asked.

Jake shook his head. "No, she's getting a copy for us."

"But—" Camille broke off. "Sorry, it's not my business."

"What were you going to say, Camille?" Max asked.

"Well, in this day and age, can't the birth certificate be faxed? What's the holdup?"

Garrett and Jake looked at each other. Finally Jake said, "It's my mother. She didn't want anyone to pressure Janelle—Mom's in no hurry to give up Chase. She said it would be better to let Janelle handle things."

"But why didn't Janelle want to rush things?" Camille asked. "I mean, I haven't met her, but I'd do anything to have Jamie close to me. If Chase is her child, why isn't she in a hurry to take him home with her?"

"I think Camille has a good point," Garrett said. "Looking at it from that direction, Janelle's behavior is highly suspicious."

"I know," Jake muttered, chastising himself. "But Mom was so convinced. There wasn't any reason to suspect the first Connor."

"Understandable," Max said.

"No. I'm supposed to be a professional," Jake protested. Camille reached and took his hand. He clasped hers with both of his, loving her touch.

"You're human, Jake, no matter how hard you try to pretend you're not," she whispered.

He frowned but said nothing.

"So," Max asked, drumming his fingers on the table, "what do we do now?"

"Does Connor number one have any idea he's under suspicion?" Garrett asked.

"No. And we don't want him to be alarmed. Smith had ID, but it could've been faked," Jake pointed out. "We'll need more proof before I'll swallow his story whole. I think he's not telling us the entire truth, either."

CAMILLE SAT quietly, listening to the men discuss Harrison Smith's strange admission. She understood their concern and fascination.

But she wanted to know about her ex-husband. She wanted to know how he'd found her. And if they thought he'd be back.

When the men paused, she broke in. "What about Vince?"

All three of them looked at her.

Jake leaned closer. "What do you mean?"

"How did he know—why was he there? Does he know where we are?"

Garrett answered. "That TV woman, Chelsea Markum, showed up at the house last night while you were in the study. Maybe your ex followed her."

"But how did he know I'd be there—or which car to follow? He couldn't see me. Jake made me hide," Camille pointed out. They hadn't convinced her she was out of danger yet.

Jake sighed. "It's probably me again. I got the SUV through the FBI. If Steve is dirty, he likely gave the license plate and description to Eckart."

Camille stared at him. "You think your contact here is the one giving him information?"

"Yeah. I'm going to have to go into town today. I need to be sure Steve is removed and my old partner takes over the investigation. And I'm not calling from here." He looked at Max. "I need a new vehicle, too. I'll pay for it, but I don't want my name on it right now."

"I can—" Max began, when the ringing of a phone interrupted them. He reached in his pocket and brought out a small cell phone. "Excuse me. Hello?"

"Can't cell phones be traced?" Camille asked.

"In some circumstances, but the conversation can always be overheard," Garrett explained. "Max is careful."

Max ended his call and turned to face them. "Harrison Smith was at the office at eight. He wants to hire my firm to discover the real identity of the first Connor. And this is strange. He also wants someone to keep an eye on that cook, Sara, at Austin Eats."

"Why?" Garrett asked.

Jake answered. "Maybe he figures, like us, that she's involved in the scam."

"Or maybe he cares about her," Camille suggested.

"Why do you say that?" Max asked.

She shrugged. "Something in his voice."

"Have you got enough men available to handle everything?" Jake asked Max.

"Yeah. We've got it covered."

"Good. Can you set up the new vehicle?"

"Yeah."

"I need you to stay here with Camille," Jake continued, assuming Max's agreement as a matter of course.

"Can't we go with you?" Camille asked. She hadn't realized she was still holding hands with Jake until he squeezed hers.

"No, that wouldn't be a good idea. Alone, I won't draw a lot of attention. With a beautiful blonde and a baby—well, we might as well have a neon sign over our heads."

"But Vince knows what you look like," she reminded him.

"I'll go in disguise...as a cowboy," he told her with a grin.

She couldn't resist responding to that smile, but it didn't allay her fears. After all, she would be able to recognize Jake in any disguise, she was sure.

"Garrett, can you run me into town?" Jake asked. "If you can, I'll leave the SUV here. We can deal with it after all this is over." He stood, releasing Camille's hand.

"When will you be back?" she asked, still anxious.

"It may take a few hours. If my old partner is here, I want to meet with him. I need to talk to the police about last night, pick up the new vehicle, see what's happening." He frowned and looked at Max. "You can stay that long, can't you, Max?"

"Yeah, if Camille will put up with me. It'll keep me from wringing that Chelsea's neck. Six hours without seeing her are six good hours."

Camille gave him a smile, but she wondered about

the vehemence in his voice. "You know her?" she asked.

Max flushed. "We've locked horns a few times."

"She's very pretty." Camille watched Max as he appeared to struggle with his emotions.

"She's a Nosey Parker. Intruding in people's lives and then broadcasting their private affairs on TV is a pathetic way to make a living!"

Garrett slapped his friend on his shoulder. "Don't let her get to you, pal. We're going to head out. If you need anything, call the ranch house."

When Garrett started for the door, Max went with him. "I need to talk to Garrett a minute," he said to Camille and Jake.

When the two men had disappeared outside, Camille reached for Jake's arm and stood beside him. "Please, Jake, be careful."

"Sweetheart, everything's going to be fine," he assured her, turning back into the man who had comforted her last night. To her surprise, he cupped her face in both hands. "Quit worrying. Vince doesn't care about me. He'll try to use me to find you, that's all. I'm as safe as can be."

"And the bullet last night? Who was it aimed at?" she asked, stiffening her shoulders. She wouldn't be talked down to like a child.

"Me," he agreed, "but only because you were with me. I'm safer if you stay here."

She knew he was right. But she wished he'd stay there with her. Safe. "All right. Just...just take care."

To her surprise, he dipped his head, and his lips

brushed hers. They touched only briefly. Just a bare grazing of their mouths. It shook Camille's world.

And startled Jake. He backed away, as if he'd seen a ghost, and rushed out of the house.

CHAPTER EIGHT

JAKE TURNED OFF the highway onto the ranch road, keeping his gaze fixed behind him. No cars were in sight, but he wouldn't be safe until he was out of sight of the highway.

And the dust had settled.

The dirt road on Garrett's ranch left a plume of dust in the air that would tell anyone where he'd driven.

The long driveway topped a hill, then descended into a treed valley. He began to breathe a little easier. Okay, so he hadn't been followed. He wasn't endangering Camille and Jamie.

It was time to face what he'd been trying to avoid all day. Thinking about his departure that morning. Thinking about being alone with Camille.

Thinking about the kiss.

He must've been out of his mind.

But she'd been so sweet, so worried. He'd only wanted to reassure her. The kiss hadn't meant anything sexually. It was a comforting kiss, to soothe her. As if she'd been a child.

Liar!

Damn, damn, damn! He wanted her. In his arms, in his bed, in his life.

He couldn't do that. He didn't know how to—to have a family. He'd rejected his own family for so many years, and in everyone's opinion, they were the best. But he'd pulled away, gone off alone, abandoned them. He had called his mother every Christmas and on her birthday, but that had been his only contact.

True, he'd been wondering, since his return to Texas, if he'd made a mistake, overreacted. He'd been so angry about his fiancée's betrayal and his father's attempts to make decisions for him, to force him in the family mold, that he'd lost control.

But that didn't mean he could mistake lust, sexual hunger, for the nesting instinct. He couldn't be that crazy.

But what about Jamie?

He almost drove the new SUV off the road when he jerked the wheel. Where had that thought come from? He was in charge of Jamie's safety. That was all. Jamie was a defenceless baby. Anyone would have feelings of protectiveness for such a little being.

Of course he cared about Jamie. He'd have to be made of stone not to. Just like he cared about Camille. But caring about the two of them didn't mean anything.

They'd be leaving as soon as Eckart was arrested.

They'd be leaving.

CAMILLE PACED the kitchen. "Shouldn't he be back by now? Are you sure nothing's gone wrong?"

"Relax, Camille. He had a long list. We would've heard if something had gone wrong."

Camille glared at Max. She was being unfair, but the longer the day went on with no sign of Jake, the more upset she became. Max was stretched out in a chair at the kitchen table playing solitaire. Perfectly relaxed.

"How do you bear it? The waiting?"

Max grinned. "You learn to pace yourself. Otherwise you'd go crazy."

"That I can believe," Camille agreed wryly. She pulled out a chair at the table and plopped down in it. Immediately she leaped up again at the faint sound of a car approaching.

"Sit down!" Max snapped, jumping to his feet. She hadn't seen him move that fast all day. Now he was a whirlwind in motion.

She didn't obey him. She hadn't given her promise to him. Just Jake. But she did keep away from the window. "Is it Jake?"

"I can't tell yet. Remember, he got a new vehicle. It's a black Explorer."

Camille nibbled on her bottom lip while she stared at Max's back. She didn't think she could bear the suspense.

"Whoever it is, he's alone," Max said. He left the window and moved to the back door, drawing his gun from the shoulder holster he wore.

"Don't shoot!" Camille pleaded. "You might hurt Jake."

"I'm not going to shoot Jake, Camille. But I have to be prepared in case it's someone pretending to be Jake."

Camille held her breath and stared at the door.

Suddenly Max relaxed. He holstered his weapon and smiled at Camille. "It's Jake."

Without any conscious decision, Camille flew past him, out the door and into the arms of a surprised Jake as he came around the new vehicle.

"Camille! What's wrong?"

She knew her reaction was over the top. But she seemed to have no control. Burying her face in his chest, she shook her head and pressed tighter against him.

"Max?" Jake took a deep breath, and Camille felt the air move through him. "What's the matter?"

Camille was totally humiliated by the laconic chuckle she heard behind her.

"She's glad to see you. Can't you tell?"

She felt Jake's hands on her shoulders, trying to ease her away from him.

"Sweetheart? Are you all right?"

"F-fine," she muttered. "I—I was worried about you."

"Everything's fine. I told you it would be."

Now she really felt like an idiot. "Of course," she managed to say, then turned and ran into the house, straight to her bedroom, closing the door firmly behind her.

JAKE STARTED after her, but Max grabbed him by the arm.

"Let her go. She's a little embarrassed right now. Give her time to recover."

"Who made you an expert on women?" Jake demanded, his gaze still on the spot where he'd last seen Camille.

"Well, it's easier when it's not your woman." Max freed himself from Jake's hold and crossed his arms, a smug look on his face.

"Wipe that smirk off your ugly mug," Jake warned. "I'm only doing my job."

"Keep telling yourself that, cowboy," Max said, still grinning. Then he turned and headed into the cabin.

Jake opened his mouth to protest, but there was no one to protest to. Besides, he wasn't sure he could put his heart into those words again. He had to admit, finally, that Camille and Jamie were more than an assignment. He'd fought any attachment, but it was there.

He followed Max into the house.

"Everything go all right today, Max? Did you make sure Camille ate a good lunch? Is Jamie doing okay?"

"Yes, Mother Jake. Camille fixed hamburgers for us. I haven't had a homemade hamburger in years. Man, it was good," he enthused, practically licking his lips.

"You made her cook? She had a bad time last night. You should've cooked for her."

Max shook his head. "There you go again."

"What?"

"I let her cook for three reasons. One, she offered, and she's a heck of a good cook. Two, I'm a lousy cook."

Jake opened his mouth to protest again, but Max

ignored him. "And third, she needed something to keep her busy so she wouldn't go crazy worrying about you."

"But I told her everything would be all right," Jake protested. Maybe Max was right. Maybe he did need some lessons about women.

Before he could ask why Max thought Camille had needed distracting, she appeared at the kitchen door.

"I'm going to start dinner," she announced, looking at no one. "Will you stay, Max?"

"Mmm, what are you fixing?"

"Barbecued chicken, mashed potatoes, tossed salad, hot biscuits." She crossed to the refrigerator and opened it.

"You know, I think I can stay for dinner. If it's not too much trouble," Max added, winking at Jake.

"Are you sure you feel like going to all that trouble?" Jake asked, then grunted as Max kicked him in the ankle. He glared at his friend.

"Of course I do. I haven't done anything all day."

Jake looked around the kitchen. "You're telling me Max cleaned up after lunch? The floor looks mopped. And I bet you did some laundry, too. As fast as Jamie gets things dirty, I know you did."

"He can't help it."

Okay, he'd told himself to keep his distance. To return to his standoffish attitude. But the welcome she'd given him wiped that resolution from his mind. And he was worried he'd offended her. She'd sounded angry when she'd defended her baby.

He crossed the room to stand behind her, cupping her shoulders. "Of course he can't help it. I know that. I'm just worried about you overdoing things. You just gave birth a couple of weeks ago.''

She sagged against his chest, and her head dropped slightly. ''It's over two weeks now. And I needed to keep busy.''

He turned her around. ''You don't need to cook tonight. I'm home.''

She lifted her chin. ''I want to. Besides, I've already promised Max.'' Then she pulled away and turned to open the refrigerator again.

Jake frowned and looked at Max. He shrugged in answer to Jake's silent question.

''I'll, uh, I'll go wash up. Then I'll come set the table. Maybe peel some potatoes.''

''That's Max's job—but I'll find one for you, too,'' she said, smiling at him for the first time.

That smile eased the pain in his stomach. His world settled into place. Camille was okay.

''Great. Be back in a minute.'' The urge to kiss her again, as he had when he'd left, almost overwhelmed him. Damn, he was going to have to watch himself.

After he'd washed up, he started back to the kitchen. Then he stopped. Without admitting the need, he turned and opened the door to Jamie's room. Tiptoeing across the floor, he looked into the little bed.

A bright-eyed baby greeted him with a soft coo.

''You're awake!'' Jake exclaimed softly. ''And you're not crying. How are you doing, Jamie?''

He reached out to touch his little fist. To his surprise, Jamie grabbed his finger, his smaller ones barely able to wrap around Jake's large one.

''Hey! You learned a new trick while I was away,''

Jake whispered, grinning. "Way to go, little one."
He liked the feeling of pride that filled him. "How
about I change your diaper and we go see Mom. She's
doing her thing in the kitchen."

Deftly he changed the baby, then picked him up
and headed down the hall to the kitchen.

"Look who decided to join us," he announced
proudly.

"Jamie? I didn't hear him cry," Camille exclaimed.

"He didn't. I, uh, I was just checking on him, and
his eyes were open. And guess what! He grabbed my
finger."

Camille smiled at him, and Jake felt as if they were
sharing something special.

"Hey, maybe he'll grab mine," Max said, drawing
closer.

"No!" Jake protested. "No, I don't think he
should. You might have germs."

"I might have germs, but you don't?" Max questioned.

"I just washed up. Besides, Jamie is used to me."
He pulled out a chair at the table, cuddling the baby
against his chest.

"Do you mind holding him while I cook?" Camille asked. "I don't need to feed him just yet."

"No problem," Jake said, but his gaze was fixed
on the little boy.

"You're just saying that 'cause you won't have to
help with dinner," Max protested.

"It's okay, Max, I don't need—" Camille began.

Jake and Max both protested at once.

"Aw, I didn't mean it," Max said.

"He didn't mean it," Jake assured her.

Camille looked at each of them. Then she smiled at Max. "Then thanks, Max. It would be a big help if you peel potatoes while I make the biscuits."

"JANELLE!"

Janelle Jones, nee Maitland, alias Davis, raised her head from the down pillow of her king-size bed. "Connor, darling, you're back. I've missed you."

She heard his angry strides through the small guest house Megan Maitland had installed them in. When he finally appeared in the doorway to the bedroom, Janelle knew she'd read his mood accurately.

"Damn it! Janelle, I almost got caught and it's your fault!"

"But, Connor, darling—"

"Can the crap! There's no one here but me," he snarled.

"Okay, fine. What's wrong, Petey? And don't even think about blaming me for any mistake you've made." She was the genius behind their elaborate con. She was the reason they were living in luxury. She was the reason the prospect looked bright for even more gain.

"Don't blame you? Why not? You're the one who didn't realize they'd make you prove the brat was yours. If you hadn't insisted on using that bitch's kid, we'd be on Easy Street!"

"Are they upset that I haven't produced the birth certificate yet?"

"Yeah, I told them it should be here soon. But then Megan asked what city the brat was born in again."

Janelle held her breath. She had already admitted to herself that she'd been shortsighted in not realizing they would want papers for the baby. But what else could've gone wrong?

"I said Las Vegas," Petey told her. "Then one of your blasted cousins said she thought you'd said something about New Mexico. The whole thing almost fell apart, right there in front of me. Damn it, you didn't warn me to be ready for that!"

"Las Vegas? You idiot!" Janelle returned angrily. "I didn't want them to know where we came from."

"Don't blame me—you didn't remind me!" he shouted.

"Well, I can't think of everything. I came up with the matching birthmarks. We wouldn't have convinced Megan so easily without them."

"Maybe not," Petey agreed reluctantly. "But all that convincing will go out the window if you don't come up with a birth certificate soon. What's the holdup?"

Janelle began pacing the room. "I haven't made any connections yet. In Vegas, I'd know who to call, but here, I have to move carefully. I don't want the authorities to know I'm in the market for a fake birth certificate."

"Well, you'd better figure out something," Petey growled, "or all this was for nothing."

"Listen here, Petey, we've been living off Megan Maitland pretty well. And she gave you that checking account with more money than either of us had seen before. So even if we have to leave today, we'd come out ahead.''

"Okay, okay," Petey agreed, losing some of his anger.

"But we're not done yet. It doesn't matter what city you told them. They'll just figure you forgot. You weren't there for the birth, anyway.''

"Yeah, that's me. I forget things.'' He grinned amiably.

"We need something to happen, though, to distract them.'' She tapped her chin. "I'll think of something. With everything that's happened already, it shouldn't be too difficult.''

Petey sprawled on the bed. "Maybe we should find that gangster guy and tell him where Jake is hiding his ex-wife?'' he suggested. "I don't like Jake. He's not friendly...though I wouldn't mind hiding out with that Camille for six months.''

Janelle gave him a glare that could reduce him to whimpers normally. She didn't like him looking at other women. "You bastard! Don't even think of taking up with another woman.''

He shoved himself farther away from her. "Quit being so mean. What did I do?''

She drew a deep breath. And tried to remember why she'd married the man. "You want to be with someone else after all I've done for you? You'd still be scratching to make it through each day if you were back in Vegas, not living like a millionaire.''

Now that all his arrogance had left him, Janelle studied Petey closely. He looked good. He felt good. He even sounded good, as long as someone else supplied the brains. That was why she'd married him. Together they made a good team. And he'd never get the upper hand, that was for sure.

She reached out to him, letting him know she forgave him. He took her hand and snuggled close. He never remained upset with her for long.

"Hey, I've got an idea," he suddenly exclaimed, startling her. "What if we tell Megan you're pregnant?"

Janelle rolled her eyes. "Why would we want to do that? I'm not."

"But I bet Megan would give us more presents."

"Not if we're getting married in a few weeks. They'll just wait until the wedding. And we may not even be here by then." He was sidetracking her from thinking of a solution.

"But if you're pregnant, Megan will be happy for us to move up the wedding day. We can tell her we've already had one baby without getting married. We want to do right by the second." With a wink, he added, "You know Mrs. Prim-and-Proper Maitland will fall for that line like a ton of bricks."

Janelle's eyes widened as she stared at her husband. "Damn, Petey, don't get too smart on me all of a sudden. That's as good as anything I've thought of."

Petey beamed with pride.

"Let's see," Janelle began. "You can tell them I haven't been feeling well because of the new baby and that's why I haven't been able to do anything about the birth certificate. Make me sound weak and miserable. You can say you should've known, 'cause when I was pregnant the first time, when you didn't know, I was a bitch. That's why we split up.'' She paused, considering their story.

Petey chuckled and leaned over to kiss her. ''Aw, baby, you're always a bitch.''

She grinned at him. ''Yeah, but they don't know that.''

After mentally reviewing the plan for a few more minutes, she ordered, ''Okay, call Megan, and tell her about the new baby and moving up the wedding.''

The conversation was much more involved and needed a lot of detail as Megan Maitland questioned ''Connor.'' Janelle held her breath, hoping Petey could carry it off.

When he finally hung up, she demanded to know the details.

''She's excited about the next baby.'' He chuckled. ''If I'd known how happy it would make her, I'd have told her we were having twins.''

''Don't get carried away, Petey. Is she willing for us to move up the wedding to next Saturday night?''

''Of course she is. With her money, it won't be a big deal. She was touched that we thought about doing the right thing as soon as possible for the second baby. And she sends her love to you. She's going to get you in to see Abby on Monday.''

''What?''

''What's the matter? I thought it was sweet.''

''You stupid bastard! I'm not pregnant! That's what's the matter!''

CHAPTER NINE

JAKE GAVE a contented sigh before he lifted the coffee cup to his lips. Dinner had been delicious. The company even better. Garrett had invited himself, promising to bring dessert. And after dinner, the three men shared kitchen cleanup while Camille fed Jamie and put him to bed.

"You haven't said a word about how things went with you today, Jake," Max accused as the three sat with their coffee.

"I didn't think I should. I didn't want to upset Camille again."

"Camille was upset?" Garrett asked, leaning forward, frowning. "What's the matter? How can we fix it?"

Again Jake wondered if his reclusive friend had a thing for Camille. He didn't want to believe that but—

"Nothing's wrong with Camille," her cool voice said from the doorway. "Nice job on the cleanup, guys. I'll retire for the night and let you chat."

"No!" Jake protested, standing. "We're not going to talk about anything you're not aware of. I mean, go if you want to rest. But if you're just trying to be polite, come join us."

Garrett nodded. "Your perspective was really helpful yesterday. And there's plenty more to talk about tonight."

"What's happened?" Camille asked, coming to the table.

"Want me to make you some herbal tea?" Jake asked. Camille had never had anything with caffeine since he'd known her.

"Thanks, but I'll fix it."

"Nope. You cooked dinner. Sit down." He turned to the kitchen cabinet where she kept the tea bags. "You go ahead, Garrett. I can still hear."

"I want to know about your day, too," Garrett said.

"Hey! I told you I didn't think—uh, I thought I should wait until after dinner." He could feel Camille's questioning look, but he concentrated on putting the water on to boil.

"Doesn't matter," Garrett said. "I'm not sure Jake even knows about the latest Connor stuff. There have been some interesting developments."

"Like what?" Jake snapped.

"The first Connor called your mother to apologize for Janelle not having the paperwork for the baby yet. He blamed her inefficiency on her being pregnant."

"She's pregnant?" Camille asked. "Has she been to a doctor?"

Garrett's smile widened. "Ah, a woman's mind. That really wouldn't have occurred to me, Camille. I assume women, mystical beings that they are, realize when they are pregnant."

"Why are you grinning like the Cheshire cat?" Max asked.

"Because, when Connor called Megan to give her the good news about the baby, she told him she'd make an appointment with Abby for Janelle on Monday."

Jake whistled. "You're right. Things are changing quickly."

"There's more. The new baby was Connor's reason for moving up the date of their wedding to a week from tomorrow night. He said they were unwed when their first child was born. They want to do things right for this second child." He patted his heart in mockery of the sentimental statement.

"Mom snapped it up, hook, line and sinker, didn't she?" Jake guessed, shaking his head.

Garrett's expression softened. "Yeah. For such an astute businesswoman, she's a real pushover when it comes to babies."

Camille seemed lost in thought. Then she looked at Garrett. "The wedding is moved up to Saturday week, and Janelle is pregnant." She shook her head. "I don't see what all that gains them."

"First of all, I doubt the pregnancy is real," Garrett said. "I forgot to add another phone call. After talking to Aunt Megan, Connor apparently turned the phone over to his beloved. She immediately called Abby's office and told the nurse not to book an appointment when Megan called because she was too busy with wedding plans to come in right now."

"Now I'm really confused," Camille said. "Why are they so anxious to marry?"

Max shrugged. "The first Connor—I like the sound of fake Connor better—never seemed like the romantic type to me. More the grab-her-by-the-hair-and-drag-her-to-the-cave type."

"Assuming he could remember where he'd parked the cave," Jake said. "He's not the sharpest knife in the drawer."

"Yeah," Garrett agreed. "Which is another reason he can't be kin to the Maitlands."

"Hey, it happens in even the best of families," Max said with a grin. "Take Jake here. All the money and position he could want. What does he do? Chucks it all and takes a vow of hardship with the FBI."

Jake managed to swallow his protest, but Camille felt no such need. Fiercely, she faced Max. "Don't you dare belittle Jake's service to his country! I wouldn't be alive today without him."

Jake reached out and took her hand, carrying it to his lips for a brief caress. "Shh, honey, Max is just teasing."

"Sorry, Camille," Max apologized immediately. "It's an old joke between us. But I'm as grateful as you that Jake has protected you."

Jake watched as her cheeks flushed and she ducked her head. "I—I'm sorry."

He wanted to wrap her in his arms. Thank her for coming to his defense, assure her that he, too, was glad he'd protected her, that he would do so with his life. He wanted to kiss her—

"No problem," Max said easily. "But back to your question about why things changed today—it has to be connected to the scam."

"Well, of course it is," Garrett agreed, sounding frustrated, "but how?"

The wall phone rang, taking everyone by surprise. Almost no one had the number.

Jake moved to answer it.

"Jake, it's your mother," the voice at the other end greeted him.

"Yeah, Mom, I know," he said, grinning at the others.

"Did you hear about Connor and Janelle's change of plans? And the new expected family member?"

"Yes, I did. Garrett's here now, filling me in."

"Garrett? I haven't phoned him yet. How did he know?"

Jake turned his back to his audience. "You know how fast news goes through this family, Mom."

"I suppose. Anyway, I wanted to be sure you and Camille would be there. After all, it's just going to be family. And if you need help picking out a gift, let me know. I can do your shopping for you."

Jake froze. Could that be it? "Uh, Mom, what are you giving Connor and Janelle as a wedding present?"

"Are you afraid I'm giving away your inheritance, son?" his mother asked quietly.

"No, Mom. I trust you." Then he fell silent, waiting.

Finally, she said, "I was going to give them a car, but I've changed my mind. Instead I'm giving them the deed to the condo Connor stayed in when he first arrived. And I think it's only fair that he receive a cash settlement." She hurriedly added, "He hasn't asked for it, Jake. Really. But he has had a hard time since your aunt Clarise died.''

"I understand, Mom. Well, I'll give the present some thought and let you know.''

"Thank you, darling. And give Camille and that sweet baby a kiss for me.''

"Mom!'' he protested. Did his mother know about his feelings for Camille? He hoped not.

Forcing his mind back to the subject at hand, he said, "Uh, Mom, have you seen Hugh Blake lately?'' The lawyer had been a friend of his father's and the family's legal adviser for many years.

"Yes, I speak to him regularly. Why?''

"I think you should run your plans for Connor by Hugh, just to get his legal opinion.''

"You're right, of course. Hugh should handle the transaction. Thanks, Jake.''

After hanging up the phone, he returned to the table. "Okay. I think I've got it figured out. Gifts.''

"Gifts?'' Garrett frowned. "You think they're going to collect the silver and hock it? I'm not sure it will be worth the risk, Jake.''

"How about the deed to one of my mother's condos, worth about three hundred thousand, and a cash settlement from his long-lost family. *Plus* the silver. They've already gotten a three-carat diamond ring and a healthy bank account.''

Max whistled. "A nice haul. Definitely worth the risk.''

"Poor Megan,'' Camille said softly. Then, as if realizing what she said, she added, "I mean, Mrs. Maitland.''

"Yeah," Jake agreed. "I can't believe my mother's been taken in by those two. I do have some good news, though."

Camille squeezed his hand, and he smiled at her.

"What's the good news?" she asked.

"Steve's out. He was recalled to D.C., and my old partner, Greg, is in charge. You remember him, don't you, Camille?"

"Yes. Can he be trusted?"

Jake stared at her. "Of course. He was my partner."

"Any sign of Vince?" she asked.

"Nope. The cops checked out the registration on the rented car." He looked at Max. "You'll love this. He used the name John Smith."

Max shook his head in disgust. "With a matching credit card, I'm sure."

"Right."

"Well, that's a dead end. But what about the guy who was parked outside the house?"

"They didn't even take him in to question him. He said he was waiting for his girlfriend, who was a maid at the party."

"Did they get her name?"

"Nope. Nothing."

"Sloppy work," Max growled.

All three men nodded, falling silent.

"But what do we do now?" Camille asked, looking at Jake.

"There's nothing else to be done tonight, sweetheart," he informed her, smiling, "except get a good night's sleep."

His cheeks reddened at his slip, afraid the other men would comment on the endearment for Camille. He rushed to deliver his next piece of news to distract them.

"I do have one more bit of news. Wait a minute." He released Camille's hand and left the kitchen to go outside. When he came back in, he had several pieces of paper in his hands.

"Greg and I did some research. Here's a picture of the real Connor O'Hara. It's not too clear, but I think you can identify him."

"Harrison Smith, as I live and breathe," Garrett said.

"I'm worried about Mom because of her attachment to Chase," Jake confessed. "We have to find out if the baby is a Maitland or not."

"Megan will probably adopt him anyway," Garrett pointed out. "We all know she loves him."

"Yeah," Max agreed. "Instead of worrying about Chase, I think we need to concentrate on the other Connor, find out what's going on. Nothing's going to stop Mrs. Maitland from loving that baby."

"Yeah, okay, you're right," Jake agreed. "And we still have Vince to deal with."

"Good." Garrett stood up. "We've bothered you long enough. Max and I will get out of here and give you some peace. Thanks for the great dinner," he said to Camille.

Max thanked her, too, then accompanied his friend to the door. He turned and looked at Jake. "You planning on staying in one place tomorrow?"

"Yeah. I missed being here today. No telling what

Jamie will learn to do tomorrow if I'm away. I'll probably come home to find him riding a bike." Jake got up, too, deciding to walk his friends to their vehicles. "I'll be back in a minute, Camille."

CAMILLE SAT at the table alone, exhaustion flowing through her in waves. Now that Jake was safely home and they would be alone, she could relax. Let go of her fears.

At least for tonight.

She'd long ago faced the fact that she might die. If she did, it would be the result of her own stupidity. She shouldn't have let Vince sweep her off her feet.

But Jamie…and Jake. They shouldn't have to pay.

The sound of the door closing and the lock being turned brought her head up. "Have they gone?"

"Yeah. Are you all right? I think today was too much for you. Especially after last night." He came over and squatted in front of her, lifting her chin. "Are you ready to turn in?"

"It's only a little after eight. Jamie will need to be fed again at ten."

Besides, even as tired as she was, she didn't think she could relax enough to fall asleep.

"Okay, how about a movie? I know a good comedy I don't think you've seen yet."

Camille's heart sank. She'd hoped— How foolish could she be? She'd hoped he'd share the rest of the evening with her. She'd missed him so much. Worried about him every minute he was gone.

But she knew what the suggestion of a movie meant. He would park her on the couch, put the movie in the VCR, as if she couldn't do it herself, then retreat to his bedroom.

She'd be left alone.

Reminding herself of her resolution to be strong, to let Jake retreat as she knew he wanted to do, she attempted a smile. "That's a good idea."

He stood and took her hand to pull her to her feet. "Why don't you go put on your pajamas and a robe while I dig out the movie."

She nodded and left the kitchen without saying anything else. If she hadn't, she would have thrown herself into his arms and begged him to hold her all night.

She was staring out the window, dressed in the T-shirt and shorts she wore as pajamas, her cotton robe on top, when Jake knocked on her door.

By the time she turned, he'd opened the door. "Are you coming? I found the movie. It's *Overboard*. Goldie Hawn and Kurt Russell. You'll love it."

"Yes, of course. Thank you." She crossed the room, brushing past him, shivers coursing through her body. She almost ran to the living room.

Once there, she settled on the sofa and picked up the remote control.

"Hey, you're not going to start without me, are you?" Jake asked from the door.

"You—you're going to watch it?"

"Yeah, it's one of my favorites. I thought it might help both of us relax."

Camille tried to repress the bubbles of happiness that were cascading through her, but knowing that Jake wanted to share the evening with her was pure heaven. "I—of course. Let me know when you're ready."

"Want some popcorn? And we have some root beer. Just like a real movie." He smiled at her as if he was offering her a forbidden treat.

And he was. But he didn't realize he was the treat. She was full from dinner. But she'd eat a gallon of popcorn if it would make Jake happy. "Of course. I'll go pop some."

"I put it in the microwave before I came to get you. It should be ready. I'll be right back."

She took deep breaths to calm herself while he was in the kitchen. They were going to watch a movie, that was all. He'd probably sit in the stuffed chair, not on the sofa with her. But his presence was a gift she would accept and be grateful for.

"Okay, I'm ready—start the movie," Jake ordered as he strolled in, balancing a big bowl of popcorn and two cans of root beer.

When he settled on the sofa only a few inches from her, she stared at him, wide-eyed.

"You don't mind, do you?" he asked. "We have to be close to share the popcorn."

"No, no, of course, I don't mind."

"It's that red button, honey," he told her kindly.

She snapped her finger down on the right button, unable to believe she was acting like such a dullard. "Of course. There, it's starting."

She sat tensely on the sofa, barely seeing the opening credits. Jake nudged her with the bowl of popcorn.

"Uh, thanks." She took several pieces.

"Oh, watch this," Jake said, pointing to the screen.

She did as he asked, but she could barely focus on the movie. Suddenly, Jake's arm came around her shoulder.

"You need to get comfortable, Camille. You're too tense. Lean against me. I really want you to watch this movie."

She edged a little closer, pretending she was pleased with his invitation. And she was. Only she couldn't trust herself to get really close to him, to let his warmth seep into her bones....

He wrapped his arm more tightly around her stiff shoulders and hauled her against him, pressing her head to his shoulder. "Relax. We're having a quiet evening at home. Watch the movie."

Gradually, the antics of the actors and the warmth from Jake's body lulled her into relaxing. Her head sank to his shoulder, and he laid his cheek on her hair.

She was in heaven.

WHEN Camille's breathing became slow and even, Jake risked moving slightly to check her eyes. Her lashes were resting on her cheeks. She appeared to be asleep.

His plan had worked. He'd realized Camille was tense. He'd wanted her to get some rest, so she'd be all right for whatever came tomorrow. It didn't hurt that he got to hold her. But he assured himself he was only taking care of her, the way he was supposed to.

He considered carrying her to her bed so she could rest more comfortably, but he convinced himself that she'd only wake if he moved her. It would be better to let her rest where she was.

Which meant he got to hold her just a little longer. Did husbands grow tired of this kind of thing? Did they get bored with the trust their women placed in them? Did they forget the promises they'd made?

He couldn't understand it, but he'd seen it happen. It might even happen to him—which was one more reason to avoid the marriage trap.

Of course, he couldn't imagine betraying Camille if she were his—ridiculous thought. He was there to protect her. That was all. She hadn't ever said she wanted anything else from him.

Yet if he were honest with himself, he'd have to admit that his feelings for her extended beyond their professional relationship—feelings that he hoped she shared. He would wait until after Eckart was in jail, then he'd tell her that—that he'd discovered how important family was. And that he wanted her and Jamie to be his family.

He pulled her a little closer, and she turned slightly, her arm going around his middle. Leaning over, he kissed her cheek.

With a sigh, he realized that he'd already made important decisions about his future—he just hadn't wanted to face them. He was ready to end his career with the FBI as soon as Eckart was captured.

He was ready to come back to his family. Back to Texas. With Camille and Jamie. He wanted to live a normal life with a sweet baby and a beautiful, loving woman.

God, please make it happen.

CHAPTER TEN

A NORMAL DAY.

Camille smiled at herself. As a teenager, she'd hated those Saturdays when she had no activities planned and her parents suggested the three of them spend the day together.

She supposed Jamie would feel the same when he was older. But not today. Today, she could spend as much time with her son—and Jake—as she wanted.

"Let's have a picnic for lunch," she suggested to Jake.

He looked up from a list he was making at the breakfast table. "A picnic? Uh, Camille, I don't think it would be a good idea to go anywhere."

"No, I meant here. We'll eat under the shade of one of those trees. Spread out a blanket. Jamie's staying awake a little longer these days. He'll like being outside."

"If that's what you want. Let me finish up here and I'll help you."

"What are you doing?" Before Jamie's birth, she wouldn't have asked any questions. But Jake had changed. He was much more open now. Besides, she felt more involved in everything that was going on.

"Trying to think of possibilities to solve our two mysteries."

"Vince and Connor?"

"Yeah. I hope there aren't any others. This family has had enough turmoil to last it a few decades."

"Me, too."

He looked up and gave her that smile that warmed her to her toes. "I've got a feeling things are coming to a head with Vince. Just a little more patience, and we'll have your life back to normal."

Abruptly she spun around, afraid he'd see the longing in her gaze. She couldn't burden him with her emotions. That wouldn't be fair. Last night, she'd slept on his shoulder until Jamie awoke. She'd awakened feeling safe, happy, warm.

He'd given her what she needed. She couldn't ask for more.

"Camille? Is everything all right?"

"Oh, yes," she assured him, a bright smile on her lips. "I'm planning our picnic. And I don't need any help. You go right ahead. It's such a beautiful day, you'll love eating outside. We'll be—we'll be just like a family."

VINCENT ECKART glowered at the dingy walls of the third cheap motel room he'd occupied since he'd followed Camille to Austin.

He was used to better.

It was all that bitch Camille's fault. A beautiful woman, true, but not worth a damn. He'd thought he could teach her to be a proper wife. Instead she'd bolted.

Now she had his kid.

He pressed his lips tightly together. Not for long. He was going to win this battle. And then he'd hightail it out of the country. He had enough money in the Caribbean to live the rest of his life in luxury. The way he was accustomed to living.

Not like this.

He hated wasting time. But he'd twisted his ankle when he'd run from that P.I. the other night. It was better now, but he figured he'd lie low a little while longer.

The phone rang.

"Yeah?"

"Mr. Eckart, it's Steve. I've got bad news. I've been taken off the case."

"Why? Did Maitland get suspicious?"

"No. He didn't like the way I handled things at the party."

The man sounded nervous, as well he should. Vince didn't tolerate screwups. "Where are you?"

Steve cleared his throat. "I'm supposed to be back in D.C. Monday morning, so I'm packing up now. I just wanted to tell you I'm sorry you weren't able to get back your wife and baby. I understand—"

"I got a little bonus for you. A thank-you." He knew this man. He was greedy. That was the only reason he'd bought Vince's story about Camille being the great love of his life. He wanted money.

"A bonus? Really, that's not necessary, Mr. Eckart."

Vince loved having an FBI agent speak to him with so much respect.

"Yeah, it is. You've been a good friend. I want you to know how much I appreciate it. I'll be right over."

"Well, if you insist," Steve agreed, excitement rising in his voice.

Vince hung up the phone and took his gun from the bedside table. He checked to be sure it was fully loaded. Then he packed his bags and called for a taxi. He'd need to find another place to stay tonight.

JAKE WAS GLAD he'd agreed to the picnic. It seemed to lighten Camille's spirits. And his, too.

He was stretched out on the blanket on his side, watching Jamie. Camille had stripped the baby down to his diaper, and he was wiggling around, kicking his feet.

"I think he likes not wearing clothes," Jake said.

"I think you're right. I've heard that babies are that way."

He waggled his eyebrows. "Maybe he gets it from his mother. Want to take off *your* clothes?" He grinned, to be sure she knew he was teasing. But he remembered catching sight of her rosebud nipple when it had slipped from Jamie's mouth.

"No, thank you," she assured him, but she was smiling.

"Darn it, Jamie, your mom won't cooperate," he complained to the baby, lightly running his forefinger over the infant's stomach.

"You won't get any complaints from him as long as I'm available every four hours."

"Yeah, he's greedy. How long will you—I mean—"

"I don't know. They say you should breast-feed at least four to six months. It gives the baby a better start."

"When does he start eating other things?" Jake needed to stop fixating on Camille's breasts. His body was beginning to react to those thoughts, and he didn't want to embarrass himself.

"Dr. Tate won't add anything else as long as he's gaining weight."

"You satisfied with Morgan? Mom's thrilled that he's joined the staff at the clinic."

"Yes, he's wonderful."

Jealousy immediately filled him. "You know he's getting married soon, don't you?"

"Of course I do. Mary Jane and I have met. Her baby is due in a couple of months. Then they plan to marry. Why?"

"You said—I didn't want you to get hurt." His cheeks were red, he could tell, but he hoped she wouldn't notice.

"I meant he's wonderful with Jamie. Next week when I go in for my three-week checkup, I need to take Jamie to see Dr. Tate, too. Can you make the appointment for me?"

"Sure."

Jamie cooed, his little mouth pursed into a circle.

"Look, he's trying to talk," Jake said.

Camille laughed. "I think you're getting a little carried away, Jake Maitland. I believe my baby's brilliant, but talking at his age is stretching it a little."

"I said trying, not talking. There's a difference," he replied with dignity.

She smiled and rolled over on her stomach, closer to Jamie.

Jake almost choked. The top of her blouse gaped, giving him an intimate view of her breasts, nestled in a white bra. The desire to remove all her clothes, to cup those warm, full breasts in his hands—

"Jake, the phone's ringing."

They were only about twenty-five feet from the back door of the cabin. Jake had left the door open so they could hear any phone calls. Now he leaped to his feet and sprinted to the house, grateful for the diversion.

"Hello?"

"Jake, Greg called Michael. The other agent, Steve something—he's been shot."

"Garrett, what are you talking about? He was shipped back to D.C. You mean he was shot in D.C.?" He hoped that was the case. He didn't want to think about what it would mean if the man had been shot in Austin.

"No. Here in his apartment. Your pal Greg thinks it might've been Eckart. The last call Steve got came from a run-down motel on the east side of town. There's a John Smith registered there."

"Damn it, why hadn't anyone— Never mind. Did Greg send men out to check?"

"Yeah. The room's been cleaned out, but the proprietor identified the picture of Eckart. So did a couple of witnesses who saw him leaving Steve's apartment."

"Can you come stay with Camille?"

"Yeah. I'll be right there."

"Thanks."

He hung up the receiver, then leaned his head against the wall. He'd wanted to believe Steve had not been dirty, just incompetent. But Eckart's shooting him pointed to his being a stooge.

Damn!

"Jake? What's wrong?" Camille asked from the doorway, Jamie in her arms.

"Uh, they located where Vince was staying. Garrett is going to come stay with you while I go check it out."

"Vince isn't there?"

"No, he's moved. But there might be a few clues. I'll feel better if I check it myself."

He wasn't sure he'd convinced her, but he didn't want to tell her Vince had killed someone. It would only add to her fears...and her guilt.

"But you seemed upset."

He smiled and crossed the room, wrapping his arms around both her and Jamie. "I was disappointed. It seems like we're always a step behind."

She leaned against him. They remained that way until Jamie stirred. He whimpered, and Jake stepped back.

"Hey, Jamie, were we squishing you?" He kissed the baby's forehead, then moved away from the two of them. "I'll go out and gather up what's left of our picnic."

It would keep her from asking any more questions.

CAMILLE FARED much better waiting for Jake's return this time. He wasn't out on his own, trying to elude Vince. Today he was one of the hunters, on Vince's heels, surrounded by other law enforcement people.

Besides, Jamie was fussy, which was unusual for her baby. His sleep today was intermittent, and he didn't nurse as much as he usually did.

"Is he all right?" Garrett asked when she came into the living room.

"I don't know. He's fussy, but I can't put my finger on anything wrong. Maybe he's just not hungry today." She wondered if the time spent outdoors could have been bad for him, but that seemed unlikely.

"I talked to Jake while you were taking care of the baby," Garrett announced. "He's on his way home."

"Oh, good." Then she realized how her remark must sound, and immediately added, "I'm just glad he's safe."

"I know." Garrett smiled at her. "It's great that he's come back home. We've all missed him."

"Do you think he'll stay?"

"You mean ask to be transferred here?"

"I suppose," Camille said slowly. "But sometimes I've thought— I'm probably wrong."

"What?"

"I've thought he might be getting tired of his job." She shouldn't have said that, but it was true. She didn't know what else he could do, but—

"You could be right."

"But what would he do?"

"Jake? There's a lot he could do. He was always

good with animals. He might want to buy himself some property, raise a few cows. Or he could buy a partnership in Max's company. Max has more business than he can handle.''

''Both of those things would involve a large initial investment,'' Camille said, frowning.

Garrett chuckled. ''Lady, you're dealing with a Maitland. Cost isn't much of a factor.''

Camille dropped her head, reminded again of the difference between Jake Maitland and herself. One of the many differences.

''Even if Jake didn't have the money, and he does, his mother would buy him whatever he wanted to have him back down here in Texas.''

''Yes,'' Camille agreed. ''She's a wonderful woman.''

''Yeah. I hate it that she's going to be hurt by this Connor business.''

''At least, in the end, she might have the real Connor in her life.''

''That's true. I just wish we could figure out how those two got that letter the fake Connor showed to Megan.''

''Have you checked their fingerprints to see if they have a record? I wouldn't think most con artists spring up overnight.''

''Yeah, Max is working on it, but we don't want to let them know we're suspicious.''

''Surely someone on Mrs. Maitland's staff goes in to the guest house to clean. It shouldn't be that hard to get something with fingerprints.''

''You're right,'' Garrett agreed. ''Good idea.'' He

looked out the kitchen window. "Here's Jake. Listen, I'm going to head out as soon as he gets in. Thanks for the suggestion, though. And the company."

"You're welcome," she said, smiling faintly.

Jake came in the door almost immediately after Garrett had gone outside. "What, no hug this time? You didn't miss me?"

She blushed. "I'm trying to be more disciplined."

"Darn. First you won't take off your clothes. Then you won't even welcome me with a hug. What's the world coming to?"

"Jake Maitland! Stop teasing me and tell me what happened."

"Not much. I searched a real fleabag motel room and found nothing." He sighed. "I talked to Greg and learned nothing. And I came home and got nothing."

His teasing made her want to fly into his arms. Suddenly she decided to give him that hug. After all, he'd asked for it. And she wanted it.

Her rush toward him took him by surprise, but he'd always been quick on his feet. As her arms went around his neck, he wrapped her body tight against his.

"Is this what you wanted?" she asked in a whisper, staring at him.

"Oh, yeah. And this, too." His lips settled softly on hers, and he nibbled, teasing and tempting.

Camille had longed for a real kiss from Jake Maitland for six months. She wasn't going to stand for half a kiss, now that they'd made it this far. Her mouth opened, and she invited him in.

An invitation he accepted at once.

His mouth slanted across hers, and he deepened the kiss, drawing her even tighter against him until her breasts were pressed against his hard chest. His hands stroked her while his lips dominated her mind and body.

Camille couldn't think, only feel. And the feelings were urging her closer and closer. Her hands were buried in his hair, delighting in the silky strands.

When his mouth lowered to her neck and one hand began working on the buttons of her blouse, she, too, began to explore, tugging his shirt from his jeans, running her hands under it to stroke his muscular chest.

Jake's breathing roughened, and his mouth returned to hers. The sweet taste of him was an aphrodisiac. With his lips alone, he was more enticing, more thrilling, more everything than she'd ever experienced before.

His desire seemed to be racing sky-high as he finally ripped the blouse apart, scattering buttons. Then he slid his hands beneath her hips, lifting her against him, burying his face in the V between her breasts.

"Camille!" he said, his tone both an exclamation and a plea.

"Yes, Jake!" she whispered, wanting his touch more than anything in the world.

Jamie cried.

The sudden light on the front porch, when she was younger, and her father's voice demanding to know what she was doing had never shocked her as much as her baby's complaint did tonight.

But then she'd never been as excited, as involved, as wanting as she was with Jake.

Though she said nothing, he slowly slid her down his body until he rested his forehead against hers. Jamie continued to cry, and he said, "I guess he's not going to turn over and go to sleep, is he?"

"No, I'm afraid not. I tried to feed him just before you got here, but he wasn't hungry."

"I think he changed his mind." His voice was laden with regret.

"I guess so." She stepped away from Jake, and he made no attempt to stop her. Of course he wouldn't, she chastised herself. He was a good, sensible man. He knew she needed to tend to her baby.

"I'll—I'll go see about Jamie."

"Uh, yeah, I'll see what I can fix for dinner. It's almost seven."

She backed out of the room, keeping her gaze on him, hoping he'd at least look at her so she could figure out what he was thinking. Was he angry that she'd thrown herself at him? But he'd been teasing her.

He didn't look at her. Instead, he headed toward the kitchen, away from her, his mind apparently already shifting from one kind of hunger to another.

DAMN, what was wrong with him? Jake demanded of himself. He'd been so glad to get home, to see Camille, that he hadn't been able to resist teasing her. He'd done some daydreaming on his way home about her rushing into his arms again.

Then, when he'd finally teased her into them, he'd

lost control. And would have had her on a bed in about two minutes if Jamie hadn't awakened.

Camille had barely recovered from giving birth. What kind of an animal was he? He hadn't even thought of what making love—having sex—would do to her. He didn't want to hurt Camille.

But he sure as hell wanted to love her.

It had seemed so natural, so right to cover her lips with his. She'd run to him, wanted him, made him feel complete. He'd promised himself he'd wait until Eckart was out of the way before he made any moves on Camille. That would be the smart thing to do.

Instead, he'd grabbed the first opportunity.

He only hoped he hadn't scared her or made her want to hide from him as well as Eckart. He wouldn't be able to bear it if she feared him.

But he didn't think she did. It seemed to him that she'd welcomed his touch as he'd welcomed hers. That she was a willing participant in what had happened.

He heard footsteps and hastily pulled open the refrigerator. He hadn't given a thought to dinner, and he'd told her—

"Jake! Something's wrong with Jamie."

He whirled, panic filling him. "What? What's wrong?"

"I'm not sure. But he's too warm. I think he's got a fever."

"Let me see him," Jake urged, reaching out for the baby. He lifted him from his mother's shoulder and put him over his, automatically patting his back.

Suddenly vomit spewed from the baby's mouth all over Jake.

CHAPTER ELEVEN

JAKE DIDN'T KNOW what had caused Jamie to throw up, but he knew what to do. "I'm calling Morgan Tate."

"But it's late. He won't be in his office."

"Nope, but they'll find him for us." He handed Jamie to Camille, grabbed the phone and dialed Maitland Maternity Hospital. As he waited for the operator, he stripped off his stained shirt.

"I need Dr. Tate. It's an emergency."

"I'm sorry, sir. You'll have to call his after-hours number to—"

"Lady, this is Jake Maitland. *You* call his number and tell him we're bringing Jamie to the hospital and he's to meet us there. You got that?"

"Yes, Mr. Maitland. I'll find him at once."

"Thanks." He never liked to use the power of his family name. But Jamie was sick. He'd use whatever he had to.

"We're taking him to the hospital?" Camille asked, her voice rising in terror with each word.

"Yeah, sweetheart, I think that's best. I'm going to go get a clean shirt. Then I'll take him so you can, uh, find a shirt with buttons."

She blushed a fiery red, but her only response was a nod.

He came out of his room two minutes later, buttoning his clean shirt on the way. Camille had grabbed the diaper bag from the baby's room, and she had Jamie strapped into his carrier.

"I'll hurry," she whispered as she ran past him.

Jake looked at the baby. His color didn't look so good. Feeling his face, Jake agreed with Camille's assessment. The baby was definitely too warm.

He crossed to the sink and found a clean tea towel. He wet it with lukewarm water, wrung it out, then carried it to Jamie. Gently he swabbed the baby's face.

Camille rushed in to see what Jake was doing. "Oh, thank you, Jake. I should've thought of that." She took the towel from him and picked up the carrier. "Can you get the diaper bag?"

"Right." He grabbed it and led the way to the Ford Explorer. He opened the back door for Camille to strap in the baby carrier.

She did so, then crawled in beside Jamie. "I'll need to ride back here so I can keep cooling him down."

He swallowed his protest. Of course, she was right. But he wanted her beside him, close to him.

"Right," he repeated. He closed the door and ran around to the driver's side. As soon as they started up the dirt road, he called Garrett to explain what had happened.

Then he turned off the phone and concentrated on getting them into Austin as fast as he could.

CAMILLE was relieved when Dr. Morgan Tate was waiting for them in the emergency room. She'd felt so helpless, worrying that her baby was sick but not knowing how to help him.

After a few questions, Dr. Tate started toward an examining room.

"We're coming, too," Jake stated, leaving no room for argument.

The doctor didn't bother to argue. "Of course."

Jake wrapped his arm around Camille's shoulders, making her feel much better. Somehow, she didn't believe anything could go wrong with Jake holding her.

She held her breath while the doctor took the baby's temperature, listened to his heartbeat and checked his eyes, mouth and ears. He didn't have to check his vocal cords, since Jamie was screaming as loud as he could.

Dr. Tate gently probed the baby's abdomen, and when he had finished his examination, he rediapered the infant and handed him to Camille.

"Okay, little boy, I'm through torturing you," Dr. Tate said with a smile.

Camille cuddled her baby, who was finally quiet but looked spent from his ordeal.

"Jamie doesn't have a fever," Dr. Tate told them. "He probably felt warm from crying. What he does have is a tendency to what we call colic—probably a result of his immature digestive system. It's very common in young babies, but most outgrow it by about three months."

The pediatrician went on to explain that colic involved fretful crying and usually occurred around the same time in the afternoon and evening. He gave Camille advice on nursing Jamie and suggested different techniques for comforting the baby during an attack. He also suggested they buy a thermometer and told them not to hesitate to bring the baby back in if he seemed listless or reluctant to nurse.

When he had finished, Jake offered his hand. "Thanks, Morgan." He nodded to the nurse. Then he put his arm around Camille, grabbed the diaper bag with his other hand and led Camille to the car.

When they reached the first all-night drugstore Jake could find, Jamie had given in to his exhaustion and was fitfully sleeping. Camille had assumed she and Jamie would go into the store with Jake.

Instead, he said, "I want you to lock the doors and stay here with Jamie." He grabbed a cloth from the glove compartment. "This isn't fashionable, but use it to cover your head so no one will recognize you. I'll be as fast as I can."

"Are you sure?"

"I'm sure."

Jake quickly found a thermometer for infants and picked up the diapers and other supplies Camille had scribbled on a list. He had cash waiting when the clerk totaled his bill. He even left a tip because he didn't want to wait for change. He could see Camille in the SUV, and he wanted to get her and the baby safely to the ranch.

"Did you get everything?" Camille asked as he slid behind the wheel.

"Yeah, everything. How is he?"

"Still sleeping, but he looks so worn-out. He moans every once in a while." She sounded as if it broke her heart.

"He's going to be okay, Camille. Morgan wouldn't have let us take him home if something serious was wrong with him." He only hoped he was right. What did he really know about Morgan Tate? He hoped his mother had done a background check on the man before hiring him.

He could be a mad scientist or a sadistic killer or—or Jake was being ridiculous. In his head, he knew he was overreacting, but his baby had never sounded in so much pain before. *Camille's baby.* That's what he meant. Camille's baby. But Jamie felt like his baby.

He pressed down on the gas, ignoring the speed limit, hoping the police weren't out tonight. He didn't want to have to explain anything. It would only take more time.

When they finally reached the cabin and got inside, Camille told Jake she was going to take Jamie into the den to feed him.

Jake immediately followed her. "What can I get you? Are you hungry? We haven't had any supper."

"Oh, Jake, I'm sorry, I forgot all about supper. I'll fix something as soon as—"

"Don't be silly. I'll fix something."

"Why don't we wait until after Jamie's in bed. Then we'll both feel better and we can fix dinner together."

Jake smiled and sat beside her on the couch. "I like the sound of that." He slid his arm around her shoulders, pulling her against him so that Jamie's little head, cushioned in Camille's arm, rested against Jake.

IT WAS ALMOST ten o'clock before they sat down to eat. Camille stared at Jake as he bit into his hamburger. That had been the fastest meal she could think of. While the burgers had cooked she'd sliced tomatoes and cheese, shredded some lettuce.

"Is something wrong?" he asked, looking up to see her staring at him.

"No, not at all," she assured him, and picked up her hamburger.

"The baby's okay, isn't he?"

Camille had checked on Jamie just before she'd sat down at the table.

"Yes, he's resting much better."

"Then?"

"I—I just wanted to say thank-you. I don't know what I would've done if you hadn't been there." Or what she would do in the future when it was only her and Jamie. She'd never felt so weak.

But she'd get stronger. She'd learn to care for her baby without Jake.

"I wouldn't want to be anywhere else, sweetheart," Jake said softly, reaching out to take her hand in his.

She blinked rapidly, hoping to hold back the tears. She didn't want him to see her weakness.

Jake leaned over and kissed her briefly. Then he said, "Eat your dinner. You've got to keep up your strength."

Maybe that was the problem. She hadn't eaten. Relief filled her, and she picked up her hamburger.

She did feel better after she'd eaten. She wasn't sure if it was because of the food or because she'd spent time with Jake, with his calm, reassuring presence.

JAKE cleared the table and rinsed the dishes, wondering if Camille was okay. She had disappeared into her bedroom, and for all he knew had gone to sleep. If they were married, he'd have felt no hesitancy about going to check on her. If they were married, he could adopt Jamie. He'd actually be his father.

He tried to dismiss such thoughts, but his mind kept coming back to the events of the evening. Even Vincent Eckart didn't interest him tonight.

The phone distracted him.

"It's Garrett. How's the baby?"

"Apparently he's got colic, but Morgan said that's not unusual and nothing to worry about."

"Is there anything I can do? Is Camille all right?"

Jake again wondered about Garrett's feelings toward Camille. He decided to make his position clear. "Look, Garrett, I'm here for Camille and Jamie. I'll take care of them."

Garrett chuckled. "Back down, Jake. I'm not trying to steal your woman. I just offered to help."

"She's not my woman!" he protested. Then he decided to be honest. "Not yet."

"You've got great taste. She's a charming lady. And Jamie is a great kid."

"Yeah," Jake agreed, smiling. Garrett was right on

all counts. All Jake had to do was convince Camille that her future and Jamie's belonged with him.

"What do you have planned for tomorrow?" Garrett asked, distracting him.

"Nothing but making sure Jamie really is okay. Besides, it's Sunday. I'm hoping all the bad guys take that day off, too."

"I hope you're right."

"Me, too. I'll call you tomorrow afternoon to tell you how Jamie is doing. Thanks for checking."

"No problem. Good night."

Jake hung up the phone, pleased that he'd made sure Garrett understood his position. He heard footsteps in the hallway and moved to the sink to finish rinsing the dishes.

"Jake, I said I'd help do them."

He turned around. "I don't mind. I thought you'd gone to bed."

She avoided his eyes. "I just wanted to sit with Jamie for a while—make sure he's okay. Who was on the phone?"

"That was Garrett. He called to see how Jamie is doing."

"How nice of him. You told him everything is all right?"

"Yeah. And I told him we weren't going anywhere tomorrow."

"I hope not. After all, you planned to stay home today, too."

The earlier events of the day seemed so far away that he'd almost forgotten the shock of Steve's death, his betrayal. "I couldn't ignore Steve's death," he explained, wanting her to understand that he wouldn't have left her if it hadn't been important.

"What?" she exclaimed with a gasp.

Jake realized what he'd done. Immediately, he tried to think of a way to distract her, to cover his gaffe. "Uh, I mean—"

"It was Vince, wasn't it?"

"Probably," he admitted with a sigh. "But don't get all sentimental over Steve. His death means he was the one supplying Vince with information."

"You're sure?" Camille asked, frowning.

"As sure as we can be without a deathbed confession."

She turned away, covering her eyes with one hand. "Vince is so horrible. How could he have killed a man?"

Jake turned her around and pulled her into his arms. Rubbing her back in soothing circles, he whispered, "Some men have no conscience. But it's not your fault." He knew she would blame herself.

"If I hadn't fallen into the man's trap, none of this would've happened."

He kissed her brow. "But you also wouldn't have had Jamie, sweetheart. You wouldn't give him up, would you?"

She looked at Jake, her eyes filled with tears. "No, but what kind of parentage does he have? If we survive, how can I answer Jamie's questions about his father?"

"Maybe Jamie will have another father, a better one. You can explain that his stepfather loves him very much—as if he were his own child." He saw himself as Jamie's father, a role he wanted more than anything.

"No, no, there'll never be another— I can't." She pulled herself from his arms and ran from the room.

Jake stood there, stunned by her reaction. There would never be another man in her life? Had he misread the signs? He'd thought for sure she had wanted him earlier that day. She'd never pulled away when he'd touched her these last few days. Had it all been his imagination?

Well, he wasn't going to accept her words without question. If nothing else, he needed to know what she was doing in his arms today if she wanted no future with him.

He stalked down the hall to her bedroom door and pounded on it. "Camille?"

"I need to rest," she called softly.

"I'm coming in," he announced, determined not to be put off.

He opened the door to discover Camille curled up on her bed, tears running down her cheeks. She scooted away from him, as if afraid he'd come after her.

"I'm not going to attack you," he snapped, irritated by her reaction. "But I think it's time we talked about what happened this afternoon."

"I didn't know Vince would kill the man!" she protested.

"Not that!" Jake said harshly. "I'm talking about what happened when I came home and you fell into my arms!"

CHAPTER TWELVE

CAMILLE LOOKED everywhere but at Jake, feeling the heat rise in her body. She didn't know if she was turning red from embarrassment or from memories of Jake's kisses, of his arms wrapped around her.

"I don't want to talk about it." *Please, God, let him go away.*

No such luck.

He stood there, glowering at her, big, handsome, sexy, impossible to resist—and impossible to claim as her own. When he'd suggested Jamie might have another daddy, she'd felt ill. The only man she could see in that role was Jake. And she knew he didn't mean himself.

"Well, that's too damn bad, because I *do* want to talk about it."

"Go away, Jake." She wasn't strong enough for a confrontation, especially one concerning her feelings for this man.

"You at least owe me an explanation," he said with a growl, looking dangerous with his hands cocked on his hips.

With a gasp, Camille came off the bed, her stance mimicking his. He had just pushed the wrong button, and she wasn't going to be nice anymore. "What did you say?"

"I said—"

"Never mind! I heard what you said. And for your information, mister, I don't owe you anything!" She cringed inside even as she said those words, but anger overrode her good sense. "After all, you've told me over and over again that you're just doing your job, right? They pay you to take care of me. Isn't that what you always say?"

"Yeah, that's what I've said," he agreed, his voice lowering, sounding more menacing as it got softer. "But that doesn't explain what happened earlier. And you know it."

He was right. So they were back to square one. He wanted to talk, and she didn't. "It was a hormonal thing," she snapped. He was a bachelor. What did he know about a woman's hormones? "They're out of whack since I had the baby."

Stunned silence greeted her explanation. He glared at her before finally saying, "So just any man would do?"

She wanted to throw herself at him, sob against his chest that he was the only man for her. But she wasn't the woman for him. She knew that. She was the ex-wife of a gangster, a man who had just murdered an FBI agent. She was the mother of that man's child. She didn't come from a wealthy background, didn't belong among his family and friends. She was his responsibility. Nothing more.

Drawing a deep breath, she countered, "Aren't women allowed to have needs? Men certainly are."

Calm, stoic Jake erupted. "Well, if that's the case, maybe I should just give good old Vince a call! Maybe sex with good old Vince was so great, you're hungering for him. Maybe that's what tonight was all about. You were pretending I was your ex-husband. Well, lady, they don't pay me enough to be a stand-in! That won't happen again!" He stormed out of the room, slamming the door behind him.

Seconds later, she heard the back door slam, as well. He was leaving. He wasn't even going to keep her safe anymore. He hated her that much.

A whimper from the other room got her attention. She hurried to check on Jamie, but her legs felt heavy and every movement was a struggle.

Jamie's little fists waved in the air, and she scooped him into her arms. She needed to concentrate on her baby now. Jake's protection had ended sooner than she'd expected, but she'd known all along that this day would come. She and Jamie were alone now—alone against the world.

JAKE PACED in the darkness. There wasn't much breeze and the day's warmth still lingered. But he didn't care. He was too upset to think about comfort.

Damn the woman! He'd wanted to talk about holding her in his arms, about the hunger he felt, his hopes for the future. Instead, she'd told him to go away. She'd told him it was hormones. She'd told him even Vince would do!

That wasn't a fair accusation, he knew. *He'd* been the one to bring up Vince. Not Camille.

Drawing a deep breath, he resumed his pacing,

though more slowly. What was happening to him? He was known for his calm, unemotional approach, his stoic shrug. It was what made him so good at his job.

Ever since he'd left Austin, withdrawn from his family, isolated himself from the wealth and privilege of his childhood, he hadn't allowed anyone to get close to him. He'd had the occasional relationship with a woman, but he'd always explained the rules. Sex was fine. Emotion—love—wasn't part of the deal. Any woman who broke that rule was quickly left behind.

But now, his fortress walls were crumbling. For six months, he'd fought his attraction to Camille—an attraction he'd recognized when he'd first met her. He'd quickly told himself it was physical, nothing else. How could it be anything else? She'd been married to a gangster. She was tainted with the same brush.

Little by little, she'd won his respect for her courage, her determination to protect her baby, her cheerful attitude in the midst of her difficulties. He'd grown close to her even though he'd tried to keep his distance.

Then he'd gone into the delivery room with her. He'd held her hand, helped her through the pain, encouraged her, held her newborn son—and, damn it, he'd fallen in love with her and Jamie both.

Or maybe he'd just finally admitted it.

Hell! And she'd as much as told him any man would do.

IT HAD BEEN a long night. Jamie had woken up more often than usual, and she'd had to strip the baby bed once. What sleep she'd gotten had been in brief snatches.

When she heard Jamie again, sometime after the sun had come up, she staggered to her feet and struggled to get to her child.

Jake was already there.

He hadn't left.

Relief flooded her sluggish body. She couldn't move, but just stood there, staring at his large form, as he bent over the baby.

He glanced over his shoulder and discovered her presence. "I think he's gone back to sleep. Why don't you do the same? I'll listen for him."

"You must be exhausted, too," she said weakly, unable to think. To her dismay, big tears plopped onto her cheeks as she was overcome with the fatigue and worry of the past few days.

He took her by the shoulders and turned her toward her room. "I think you were up most of the night. Go on back to bed. I'll call you if I need you."

Exhaustion urged her to do as he said. But she stopped as she reached her door. "Jake?"

He was leaning over the crib, tucking the blanket securely around Jamie. What a wonderful sight. Jake and her little baby. "Jake, thank you for coming back."

Then she shut the door and almost fell into bed.

JAKE REMAINED staring at the closed door. She thought he'd left her? Left her and Jamie alone, unprotected? He'd never do that. Even if he didn't love the two of them, he'd never abandon an assignment.

But honesty forced him to admit she might've had reason to think such a thing. He'd slammed out the back door, and he hadn't come in until an hour ago. He'd gotten weary of his pacing and had sat down in his SUV to think. And had fallen asleep.

When he'd come in, he'd found a heap of baby sleepers and crib sheets piled on the floor in Jamie's room. Camille was meticulously neat, and Jake knew she would never have left such a mess if she hadn't been exhausted.

Which only increased his guilt.

Now he put the laundry into the washing machine and set out the breakfast dishes. By the time the coffee was ready—decaf for Camille—he could hear Jamie starting to fuss. He hurried into the bedroom to see if he could buy a few more minutes' rest for Camille.

"Good morning, little guy," he whispered, gently cradling the baby and kissing his forehead. "I know it was kind of rotten of me to run out on your mom last night, but it won't happen again, I promise you."

Jamie's big eyes blinked several times as he tried to focus on Jake.

"You know, Jamie," Jake went on, picking up a fresh diaper, "when you get older, there's lots more I can teach you. How to ride a bike. I'll get you a horse, too. How to play baseball. Lots of guy things. We men have to stick together, you know."

For the first time since his argument with Camille, Jake felt better. Maybe all wasn't lost. He just had to be patient, to find Eckart. Then he and Camille could talk about the future.

Until then, he'd keep his conversation reserved for Jamie. The boy seemed to understand Jake a lot better than his mother did.

VINCE WAS IN yet another cheap motel room.

It wasn't fair. He could pay for the best Austin could offer, but he couldn't afford to draw attention to himself. Those stupid feds might actually manage to arrest him if he didn't lie low.

They thought they were so smart. But he'd outsmarted them at every turn. Now he had Maitland's new vehicle marked. He'd hung around Steve's apartment, hiding nearby, knowing Maitland would show up. When he had, Vince had noted the make, a Ford Explorer, and he'd memorized the plate.

He'd made arrangements for another vehicle so he wouldn't be immobilized for long. And when he caught sight of Maitland again, he'd tail him to wherever he was hiding Camille.

He just had to think of a way to lure Maitland into town. Then he'd have the upper hand.

Damn her! She wasn't going to win.

DURING ONE of Jamie's naps, the phone rang. Jake grabbed it quickly, hoping it wouldn't awaken Camille or Jamie.

"Darling, it's your mother."

"Yeah, Mom. What's up?"

"Morgan just told me about Jamie. How is he?"

"I think Morgan was right. It's just colic. We probably panicked a bit because he's never cried like that before."

"That's only natural—first babies are always a learning experience. Is there anything I can do?"

"No, thanks, we've got everything under control. Camille was up most of the night so she's sleeping right now."

"Darling, I'm so proud of you. You're going to make an excellent daddy to that little boy."

Her words surprised him, as did the sense of pride that filled him. He remembered his conversation with Jamie with a grin. "Yeah, I am, aren't I?" he agreed. Then he hastily added, "Nothing's settled yet, Mom, so don't—"

"Say anything? I know. I can be discreet." She paused, then went on. "Can I ask you something?"

"Sure." He hoped she wasn't going to ask about his relationship with Camille. He wasn't too sure about it himself.

Instead, she broached another subject. "What do you think of Connor?"

Jake caught himself just in time. He'd almost asked, "Which one?" Instead he said, "Uh, why do you ask, Mom?"

"I knew it," she muttered. "You don't like him, either."

"I didn't say that," Jake protested.

"You didn't have to. None of you kids like him."

"Mom, you're being silly," he said gently. "It's just taking time to adjust to him and Janelle. We'll come around." Anxious to change the subject, he said, "Hey, I've got news that I think might please you."

"What's that?"

"I'm thinking about leaving the Department, coming back home." He couldn't hide the rush of emotion he felt.

"Oh, Jake! Jake, that's wonderful news! Oh, I can't wait to tell everyone! Oh, my, I—"

"Mom! Uh, could you keep it a secret for a few days? I'm not ready to go public with it yet. I have to clean up the business with Eckart first."

"Oh, of course. You and Camille need to tie up the loose ends before—oh, Jake, I'm so thrilled, I'm crying. Thank you, darling, you've made me so happy!"

And made him feel like a selfish heel. He hadn't meant to hurt his mother by leaving the way he had. Or his father. He hadn't realized how much she would care. He thought about Jamie. What if he struck out on his own one day, turning his back on everything and everyone familiar?

The sudden pain he felt was ridiculous. Jamie was two, almost three weeks old. He couldn't even crawl, much less walk. But Jake knew, as sure as he knew he'd take his next breath, that he wouldn't want to let Jamie walk out of his life, no matter what his age.

He hoped he would show the same patience and faith his mother had, if the time ever came.

WHEN CAMILLE woke, she immediately checked her watch. Almost two o'clock? She jumped from her bed. She'd slept four hours! She ran to the nursery, but the bed was empty. Irrational fear flooded her. Had Vince found them? Had he taken her baby away?

She ran through the house, her mind racing ninety

miles a minute, until she came to an abrupt halt in the living room. There, on the sofa, was Jake, sound asleep. On his chest was a sleeping Jamie, anchored by Jake's big hand on his back.

The adrenaline that had been charging through her faded away, and she sank into the nearest chair, her knees suddenly weak. Even as she watched, Jamie stirred, wiggling and making quiet baby sounds. Jake's hand, as if operated by a puppeteer, patted her baby's back until Jamie settled into sleep again.

A warm feeling flooded through Camille. He'd make the best daddy in the world. Too bad he wouldn't be Jamie's daddy. But one day she'd tell her son about the brave man who'd cared for him.

She rose and crossed the room. Very gently, she lifted Jake's hand so she could take Jamie. Jake awoke at once.

"What are you doing?"

"I'm going to put Jamie in his bed so you can rest."

"He's fine. He likes sleeping here. He can hear my heartbeat, I think."

"But it might be dangerous if you turned over in your sleep," she said, trying to find a reason to take Jamie to his bed.

Jake's gaze filled with concern. "Yes, of course. Sorry, I didn't think."

"Jake, I didn't mean—" she hurriedly began, realizing she'd hurt his feelings. "You've taken wonderful care of him."

Jake ignored her conciliatory words as she lifted the baby from his chest. Sitting up, he swung his legs to the floor. "I'm amazed he slept so long. He must have been catching up on his sleep, too."

"I'm glad, though I have to admit I'm ready to feed him now, whether he's hungry or not."

Jake glanced at her engorged breasts, and Camille felt them tighten in response. Without another word, she hurried out of the room.

JANELLE PACED the living room of the guest house. Something was wrong. She wasn't sure what, but she had a gut feeling that something was out of whack. And she had no idea how to figure out what it was. How could she? She was stuck in this prison, trapped by her lies.

But relying on Petey for information was useless. Besides, she didn't trust him. He liked women. It wouldn't be the first time he'd betrayed her. She usually kept him on a short leash, but it wasn't easy when she had to let him out on his own. After the party at Megan's house, all he'd wanted to talk about was some strange woman who had accompanied Jake.

She'd actually gotten jealous of this Camille person—which had made sex so much more exciting. A reminiscent smile lingered on her face as she recalled their evening. Then she hurriedly brought her attention to the present. She was uneasy about their situation.

Megan had asked Petey to come to lunch. Janelle didn't think the woman suspected anything yet. She was remarkably open for someone with her power and wealth, Janelle thought scornfully. There was no doubt that wealth always fell into the wrong hands.

If she had Megan's money, she'd keep everyone on their toes.

Well, she'd have a share of the Maitland fortune before she was through. She deserved it. Her father was a Maitland, too, even if he'd taken his inheritance and wasted it all. She shouldn't have to pay for his stupidity.

All they had to do was hold out for another week. She should be able to stall on the birth papers. She knew the only reason Megan wasn't pushing her harder was that she loved having that little kid in the nursery.

The front door opened, making her spin around. "Petey, what—" She stopped abruptly as she saw a woman behind him.

"That's Janelle's pet name for me," he told the woman with a flirtatious smile that made Janelle grind her teeth. The woman wasn't a beauty or all that young, but she was female, and that was Petey's main requirement.

"You remember Annie, don't you, Janelle? She helps out in the kitchen. Megan sent her over to see about you. And we brought you some leftovers, too."

He beamed at her, as if she should be thrilled. Leftovers! While he'd been waited on hand and foot! But she had a role to play, and she was darn good at it. "Why, thank you so much, Annie. That's so kind of you." The bitch. She didn't want to be there any more than Janelle wanted her there.

"I'm delighted, Miss Davis. Before I serve your lunch, may I get you both something to drink?"

Petey responded at once. He was really enjoying

being waited on. ''A Scotch and soda for each of us,'' he said with a grin.

It took Janelle a moment to realize why Annie gave her a funny look. ''Oh, no, Connor, darling. You forgot I might be—well, I'd better stick to iced tea.'' She shot Annie an apologetic look, as if she hated to cause any trouble.

She was rewarded by Annie's approving smile. It was none of the bitch's business, Janelle thought, her irritation hidden behind a smile.

The woman brought their drinks, and Petey patted her rear as she served him, giving her a warm thank-you. Annie appeared shocked by Petey's action, and Janelle ground her teeth in frustration. She'd have to threaten him again. The women he'd met here weren't Vegas hustlers.

By the time Annie was ready to go, Janelle was definitely on edge. Just as the woman was packing up the dishes she'd brought with her, Janelle noticed she'd included their two glasses. ''Why are you taking the glasses? They belong here.''

The woman turned, a smile on her face. ''Yes, they do, but I found chips on these two, so I'll send over some replacements. Mrs. Maitland would skin me alive if I didn't keep things in tip-top shape.''

Then she scooted out the door.

Petey closed it behind her, a big grin on his face. ''Man, I love being rich. Isn't that perfect? A nick on a glass and it gets tossed.''

''Were those the glasses we just used?'' Janelle suddenly asked.

''Nah. I'm sure she washed those and put them

away. She's very efficient. Megan doesn't hire slackers." The self-satisfied smile on his face irritated her even more.

"You've got to keep your hands off the help," she snapped, determined to wipe that look off his face.

"Annie doesn't mind," he assured her. "You're just jealous, but you know I love you best." He leaned in for a kiss and grabbed one of her breasts at the same time.

She ignored his sexual come-on. "What did Megan want?"

"The pleasure of my company," he assured her. Then he squeezed her breast tighter. "Come on, baby. I've been good all day. I deserve a reward." His mouth covered hers, his tongue thrusting inside her mouth as his hands began tugging down her shorts and panties.

"Petey!" she protested. Then she gave in to his demands. Later. They'd talk later.

THE REST OF Sunday, Jake and Camille only exchanged words when necessary. They both turned in early. Jamie had a brief spell of fitful crying, but they took turns walking around the cabin with him, and it soon passed. He even managed to sleep another four hours straight.

When Jake got up Monday morning, he felt a sense of doom that made him tense. Things were coming to a head with Vince, he felt sure. He wished he could say the same for the Connor situation. But as yet, they had no idea how the first Connor had come by the letter he'd shown Megan.

Jake was sitting at the breakfast table, trying to plan their strategy, when Camille came into the kitchen.

"I didn't thank you for doing the laundry yesterday," she said as she crossed the room. But she didn't look at him. She'd avoided any eye contact with him since yesterday evening.

"No problem," he said, lifting his coffee cup to take a sip.

"Would you care for more coffee?" she asked, playing the perfect hostess.

"Sure." He shoved his cup in her direction. He didn't need any more coffee, but he figured he could play this game, too. He wanted to prove he could out-polite Miss Perfect any time.

She poured his coffee before she began working at the kitchen cabinet.

"What are you doing?" She'd already cooked him a big breakfast only an hour ago. "I thought I'd make some cookies." She kept her back to him.

"Why? Jamie is too young to want any." He sounded grouchy, he knew, but her starchy behavior, as if they were strangers, irritated him.

"Jamie's not the only person in the house."

"You're hungry for cookies? Why didn't you say so? I could've brought some home from a bakery while I was in Austin on Saturday."

His words seemed to upset her. "*I* don't want cookies! I was baking them for you. I wanted to do something nice to say thank-you for—for helping out yesterday. Is that so terrible?"

He stared at her. Her eyes were glistening, as if

they were full of unshed tears. Why? Did she care what he thought? Did she want to please him?

It was a heady thought. Especially after she'd told him her response to him had been nothing but hormones.

He stood and took several steps toward her. "How are your hormones this morning?" he asked suddenly.

She whirled, spilling flour all over the floor. "What?"

"You heard me," he told her, taking the cup of flour from her hand and setting it on the counter. "I want to know if you have any needs this morning that I can help you with." He crowded her against the edge of the counter. He was behaving badly, he knew. But he couldn't seem to help himself. Always-in-control Jake was suddenly out of control.

"I've got to tell you, lady," he whispered, leaning closer, "cookies aren't what I'm hungry for."

ten it when he'd rung her. When Jake had made
promise, though, what he'd meant to tell her was
that he'd keep the handcuffs tucked in his pocket.
Just her luck, he hadn't had a chance to fill her in
before—

CHAPTER THIRTEEN

JAKE HAD PROMISED himself he'd be patient, so he
should have been pleased when the phone rang, forcing him to stop taunting Camille. But he wasn't.

He wanted her. In every way possible.

When he finally hung up, he turned to stare at her.
She'd returned to her cookie-making after sweeping
up the spilled flour.

"How are the cookies coming along?"

"Why?" she snapped, stubbornly keeping her gaze
fixed on her hands. "Have you changed your mind
about eating them?"

"Look, I'm sorry about what I said. The frustration—I mean, we've been chasing Eckart for almost
seven months."

"I know."

Her quiet response made Jake feel like a jerk. Camille was the one who'd been hurt most of all by their
inability to catch her ex-husband. Before he could
apologize, she distracted him with a question.

"Who was on the phone?"

"Garrett. He wanted to thank you for your suggestion about getting prints from Connor and Janelle."
He waited for a response, but other than a quick nod,

she ignored him, turning her attention to the cookie dough.

"Why didn't you tell me you talked about that?"

"We were just having a casual conversation. I suggested the two wouldn't suspect anything if one of the household staff took care of getting something with fingerprints."

"Apparently, you were right. The FBI is running the prints now, but we've got another clue."

"What?" she asked, turning around, voluntarily looking at him for the first time that morning.

He took a step forward, finding it difficult to concentrate on such a distasteful subject as Connor and Janelle when beautiful Camille was staring at him. He reached out to cup her cheek, so desperate to feel her warmth he couldn't resist.

"What clue?" she asked again, drawing back, letting him know he wasn't forgiven.

"Uh, Janelle called him Petey when he entered the guest house. She didn't know Annie was with him for a second or two."

Camille grimaced. "What an unattractive name for a grown man. It makes him sound…weak."

"Yeah," Jake agreed, moving a step closer. "Of course, Jake's a strong name."

She shifted her gaze. "Yes, it is. And you're a strong man. Dedicated to your work." She whirled away and moved to the door of the refrigerator. "I need some butter."

He had to back off. He was making her nervous. "Is butter good for us?"

''Probably not,'' she said, smiling briefly, ''but it sure tastes great. Besides, I'll use half vegetable oil.''

''So I can eat twice as many.''

She grinned, and her smile ratcheted up his desire for her one notch higher. Then she reached over and patted his flat stomach, and he audibly gasped. Embarrassed, she jerked her hand back. ''Uh, I think you can afford a few extra calories.''

He wanted to tell her again that cookies weren't what he wanted. He wanted to hold her in his arms again, his mouth on hers, but he'd promised patience. He'd promised.

''Yeah.'' He cleared his throat. ''Um, when do you take Jamie back to see Morgan?''

''I need to call him. Tomorrow is my checkup with Abby. My three-week checkup,'' she added when he looked alarmed. ''I thought maybe I could have Jamie checked at the same time, to save an extra trip into town.''

Jake frowned. ''Yeah. I hate the risk when you leave the ranch. Want me to ask them both to come out here?''

''No. I don't want to cause extra trouble. Surely a trip to the hospital will be safe enough.''

He didn't want to remind her of Eckart's hostage-taking at the hospital in April. Vince had threatened the children at the Maitland day care if he didn't find out where Camille was. Jake decided he'd alert Michael to the need for increased security on Tuesday. ''What time's your appointment?''

''I don't know. I need to call Abby's office. We didn't set a time when Jamie was born.''

Jake shoved away from the kitchen counter. "I'll call both of them and set things up while you finish the cookies."

"Thanks, Jake. You take such good care—I mean, you do such a good job." She hurriedly stared at the cookie dough as her cheeks reddened.

It wasn't a job to him, and they both knew it. He wanted her to admit it. Taking her chin between his thumb and forefinger, he corrected her. "I take good care of you and Jamie." Then he brushed his lips over hers before quickly walking out of the room.

He had to get out of there before he forgot to be patient.

TUESDAY was going to be a hell of a day, Jake surmised. They should have a report on the fingerprints this morning, and both Jamie and Camille were going to the doctor today.

He lay in his bed, staring at the ceiling. Would Camille be her old self this morning? Last night, she'd kept quiet, refusing to look at him, seeking her own room as soon as supper was over.

He'd heard Jamie once in the night, but he hadn't gotten up to help. He couldn't substitute for a nursing mother. Besides, Jamie seemed to be sleeping five or six hours at a time now, so it should be easier on Camille.

With a sigh, he swung his legs out of bed and headed for the shower. He'd clean up, then fix breakfast. They were going to have a busy day.

The morning sped by. After the adults' breakfast, Jamie awakened, demanding his own. After she fed him, Camille brought him to the kitchen, and Jake filled the little plastic tub she had started using for bathing her son.

Jake loved watching the baby's bath.

"Do you want to hold him while I get a new outfit for him?" she asked.

She'd been so cool with him lately, Jake was relieved she'd at least trust him with Jamie. "Sure." He cuddled the infant to him, talking softly. "Hey, Jamie, ready for a swim? Mom's going to get ready, then you get to dive in." He swayed back and forth to entertain the baby, but Jamie started closing his eyes.

"Hey, he's going to sleep," Jake exclaimed.

"Well, quit rocking him," she suggested dryly, her gaze on the two of them.

Jake stilled at once. "Oh. I hadn't thought of that."

After a quick trip to the nursery, Camille came back with the baby clothes she'd gotten and reached for her son. Jake stood beside her, drawing in her scent, ready to lend a hand if she needed it.

"Will you throw away this diaper?" she asked.

Diaper duty. He'd hoped for something better. "Sure." By the time he'd turned around from the trash can, she had Jamie in the water.

"He sure does like his bath, don't you think?" Jake commented.

"As far as I can tell. At least he's not crying."

"Do some babies do that?" Jake asked, surprised.

"Yes, or so I've heard." She took a soft washcloth and began wiping Jamie's little body. Then she rinsed him. "Would you pour a drop of shampoo on the washcloth?"

"Sure."

After she rinsed away the shampoo, she lifted Jamie out of the water. "Can you put the towel around him?"

Jake slipped the hood of the baby towel on Jamie's head and wrapped the towel around his body. Then he lifted him out of his mother's grasp. "Mmm, there's not much that smells better than a clean baby," he said with a smile.

His words pleased Camille. She said, "If you want to dry him off and dress him, I've got everything ready. I can clean up here."

"I'll do the cleaning up. You dress him."

She nodded in gratitude and took Jamie from him. As she reached the door to the kitchen, he stopped her. "We make a good team, Camille."

She didn't turn around, but she paused. Then, with a sigh, she said, "Yes, we do. I'm going to put Jamie in his bed after I dress him and then get in the shower myself. If you hear him crying, could you check on him?"

"Of course." He'd rather check on Camille. In the shower. In his mind's eye, he saw her standing naked beneath the spray, her head thrown back, the water splashing on her soft skin.

As his body began to respond to that image, the phone rang again. "Damn, we're getting a lot of calls for a number that's supposed to be secret." He snatched up the receiver. "Hello?"

"Hi, it's Garrett. I've got information. Okay if Michael, Max and I come out?"

"Sure. I'll put on some coffee." And he could fill a plate with those notorious cookies Camille had finished baking yesterday afternoon.

Strange, he wasn't even curious about the information. It had to do with the Connor situation, he was sure. But he was more interested in Camille. In their situation.

After he plugged in the coffeepot and put cookies on the table, he decided he should check on Jamie before the others got there. He tiptoed down the hall and opened the door to the nursery, trying to ignore the sound of running water.

Jamie was tucked in his bed, eyes closed, sleeping soundly. Jake pulled his blanket more snugly around him. Sometimes, while he slept, he kicked his cover loose. Since it was summer, he wouldn't freeze, but the air-conditioning could give him a chill.

The sound of a truck alerted him to the others' arrival, and he hurried out of the nursery, closing the door behind him. He reached the back door just as Garrett was about to knock.

"Come on in," he invited, waving the three men toward the kitchen. "The coffee should be ready, and Camille baked cookies if anyone's hungry."

They all looked ravenous, Jake decided, as their eyes lighted up and they hurried to the kitchen. "Didn't you eat breakfast?"

"Sure," Max said, already biting into a chocolate-chip cookie. "But that was hours ago. Besides, I don't often get home-baked cookies."

"Yeah," Garrett agreed. "You're the only one with a woman."

"Damn it, Garrett, you've got a housekeeper! Quit acting like you're all alone."

"Yeah, but she doesn't look like Camille," Garrett teased, a big grin on his face.

Jake felt his own face turn red. "That doesn't have anything to do with making cookies."

The other three men just grinned at him. Jake crossed to the cabinet and got down coffee mugs.

When they were all seated around the table, Jake asked, "Okay, what's the news? The fingerprints?"

"The fingerprints. They prove that Janelle Davis is an alias."

"We suspected that much. That doesn't tell us anything," Jake replied.

"Jake?" a soprano voice called.

"Aha, the cookie maker," Garrett said, grinning. "Invite her to join us."

"She just got out of the shower," Jake said, distracted as he got up from the table.

"Even better," Max growled with a huge grin.

Jake snapped his head around. "What did you say?" He hadn't meant to sound so ferocious, but he suddenly realized what all three were picturing in their minds. Because he'd done the same thing. He wanted to slug all of them.

"Nothing," Max said, wearing an angelic expression.

"Don't mess with Camille, you hear me? She's a lady." Then he hurried from the room.

Garrett turned to Max. "You'd better watch out.

You almost lost your front teeth. Jake is as strong as a mule.''

"And just as hardheaded," Michael added.

"And head over heels in love with Camille, I know," Max finished. "I just don't understand why he hasn't made his move. They've been living together for almost seven months. Do you think he's kept his hands off her all this time?"

Garrett and Michael exchanged a look. Then Michael said, "Jake doesn't usually mix business with pleasure. I think until recently he's tried to look on Camille as strictly business."

"Yeah," Garrett agreed. "But since she's had the baby, things have changed."

"Maybe it was seeing her in that green dress the other night," Max speculated. "She was a knockout."

"She was, but don't say that in front of Jake," Garrett warned.

"Don't say what?" Jake demanded from the door.

"Nothing," all three men hastily said in unison. Then they leaped to their feet as they saw Camille behind Jake.

"Camille, these are great cookies," Garrett said, pulling out a chair at the table. "Come join us."

"Thank you." She sat down, leaving Jake to scrounge up another chair. "Jake said you had information."

"Yeah, about the first Connor and Janelle," Michael said. "Have you met her?"

"No, she didn't attend the party, and that's the only time I met—either Connor."

Jake scooted her over a little and settled his chair right next to her. He glared at his companions, as if daring them to say anything. "Okay, let's have it. What else do the fingerprints tell us?"

"We don't know the guy's real name, other than Petey—he hasn't been arrested before," Michael said. "But we think Janelle's the brains behind the operation. We're fortunate. Her prints were on file for shoplifting when she was eighteen. If she'd been a year younger, we wouldn't have gotten any information."

"So far, you've told me nothing," Jake said in frustration.

Michael grinned. "We're spinning out the story to tease you. You're going to really be surprised. Want to guess?"

Jake knew Michael. As a child, he'd learned that Michael loved to tease. If he pressed him for an answer, Michael would delight in prolonging his response.

"Nope. And you'd better step on it. Camille has a doctor's appointment this afternoon."

All the men stared at her, and she turned a bright red. "Nothing's wrong. It's my regular checkup after having a baby."

"Oh, good." Garrett patted her hand. "You had us worried there for a minute."

Jake glared at him.

Michael cleared his throat. "Okay, here it is. Somehow Janelle found out about the real Connor's relationship to your family because she's family, too. Janelle Davis was born Janelle Maitland—your cousin."

CHAPTER FOURTEEN

"WHAT?" Jake demanded, leaping to his feet. "You're kidding."

"Nope," Michael assured him. "Her father was your uncle Robert, your brother R.J. and sister Anna's real dad. He moved to Vegas and remarried. Had four children. Janelle is the oldest."

"Her fingerprints told you all that?" Camille asked, her gaze wide.

"No," Jake assured her. "But her name gave them the connection. Someone's been doing some digging to get the rest of it."

The other men nodded.

"Right as usual, Jake," Garrett commented.

Jake looked puzzled. "Still, how did Janelle get a letter in Clarise's handwriting, since the real Connor claims to have one, too—from the lawyers?"

"You haven't seen the letter, have you?" Garrett asked.

Jake shook his head. "I told you. Mom said there was personal info in there that she wanted to keep private for the time being. As a matter of fact, I can't be positive the first Connor's letter was from Clarise. Basically, Mom made us take her word Connor had proof that confirmed he was her nephew, Clarise's son." He eyed Michael closely. "Does Mom know about Janelle yet?"

Michael shook his head. "That's really why we're here," he confessed. "Someone needs to tell her."

Since all three men were staring at him, it wasn't hard for Jake to figure out who they thought should do the job.

Camille put the question into words. "You want Jake to tell her?"

They nodded again.

"When?" Jake asked. "Shouldn't we wait until we find out exactly what they want? I mean, until we catch them doing something we can make stick?"

Michael's lips firmed in a straight line. Garrett rubbed his forehead. Max looked from one to the other.

Camille leaned forward. "Haven't they done enough?"

"Yeah, I guess," Jake said. "But I want something that will put them away for a long time."

"The baby—" Camille said, then suddenly stopped. "Jake, if you can wait until you know whether Chase is really part of your mother's family, won't it make it easier on her?"

"Yeah, if he is," Jake agreed. "But I don't think he can be Smith—O'Hara's kid. He didn't have any doubts about his lack of involvement. You heard him."

"You think we should wait?" Michael asked, frowning. "Isn't that taking an unnecessary risk?"

"They don't suspect anything, do they?" Garrett asked. "As long as they don't sniff out anything, it should be all right. And I agree with Camille. That will be easier for your mother."

"Maybe," Jake said, a frown on his face, "but I think we should at least warn Mom that we have doubts about Connor, the first Connor, right away."

Camille looked thoughtful. "My doctor's appointment and Jamie's are at two today. Do I need to change that? Jake, you were going to take Jamie to Morgan while I saw Abby."

"No!" Jake said immediately. He didn't even need to consider her question. He'd take care of Jamie. Then he'd deal with the Connor situation. Damn, he was glad that man wasn't really a part of his family. He only hoped his mother would be glad, too.

"So, shall we join you?" Garrett asked. "Talk to Megan afterward? How long will it take for Jamie to be checked?"

Camille shrugged. "If he's first in after lunch, it shouldn't take more than ten or fifteen minutes, I think."

"I'll make sure he's first," Jake said. "We'll get there a few minutes early, and I'll talk to the nurse."

"Pulling rank, huh?" Max teased. "I knew rich people did that."

"All right," Michael agreed, standing. "It's almost ten-thirty right now. We'll see you at the hospital a little after two."

"WHERE have you been?" Janelle demanded as Petey walked through the front door. Her glare wiped the grin off his face. "You didn't call attention to your-self, did you?"

"Hey, I'm a member of the family. I can throw some weight around if I want."

"Petey, what did you do?" She'd been growing more tense all morning.

"Nothing," Petey returned, irritation on his face. "The only problem wasn't caused by me. It was that Smith fellow."

"What Smith fellow?"

"You know, I mentioned him. He was at the party. The one whose daughter is pregnant and he's check-ing out the hospital to see if it's good enough for his precious new grandchild." Petey snorted in disgust. "Damn well better be. After all, it belongs to the Maitlands. We only have the best."

"You do remember you're not a Maitland, don't you?" she asked dryly, distracted by his belief in their fantasy.

"I'm almost married to one. Close enough to spend the money, anyway. Hey, I stopped by the mall on the way here. Bought me a couple more suits."

"Petey! You've already bought more suits than you'll wear in your lifetime!"

He grinned. "Don't fret, babe. I bought you some-thing. From Victoria's Secret."

"Humph! That's for you, too."

He moved toward her, probably to convince her his gift was for her, but something about his earlier words niggled at her. "What problem did Smith cause?"

"Nothing much. It was kind of funny. I asked one of the waitresses at the diner for a soda. She called my name, and the Smith guy turned and answered. Boy, was he embarrassed."

"He answered to the name Connor?" Janelle demanded.

"Naw, I don't let employees call me Connor. She called me Mr. O'Hara, with respect."

Janelle ignored his bragging. Her blood pressure was rising. "Didn't you find it strange Smith answered to O'Hara? Have you met this man?" Janelle was getting a headache, and she didn't ask nicely.

"Well, hell, babe, I said I did. At the party. He almost passed out. Ruined my chance to get close to Camille." As if he'd realized what he said, he laughed nervously. "Just teasing."

"Why did he almost pass out?" Why hadn't the idiot told her this before?

"Who knows. Megan was introducing him to all of us and he went white as a sheet."

"Describe him!"

"Stop ordering me around, Janelle. You're acting like you're the general and I'm the private. I'm a Maitland, too. I'm the reason everything's going well. Just back off."

"You imbecile!" Janelle screamed, surging to her feet. "Something's wrong here. Describe him. Is he doddering and old? Gray-haired?"

"No, he's not! In fact, everyone was talking about how young he looked. Some of the women thought he was good-looking, but he didn't do anything for me.'' He grinned, seemingly amused at his little joke.

''Is he dark-haired, handsome?''

''I told you some of the ladies thought so. Has a ranch in Montana. You know how women are about cowboys.''

''Damn it to hell! It's Connor!'' Janelle exclaimed, falling back onto the sofa, her face white.

For the first time, Petey's concern matched hers. ''What? Why would he come here? You never said he'd show up. You must be wrong!''

''Think back. When did he almost pass out? Who was being introduced?''

Petey stared into the distance. Then he turned to gape at Janelle. ''Megan had just introduced me.''

''Damn, damn, damn! We've got to get out of here!'' She jumped up and headed toward the bedroom. ''Come on, Petey, don't sit there. We may not have long.''

He hurried after her. ''You think he'll tell?''

''Hell, yes! Wouldn't you?''

''I'm sure Megan doesn't know. She won't let them hurt me. I know she won't.''

Janelle stared at him. ''Petey, sometimes you are so stupid! She may not know right now, but when she finds out you've tricked her, she'll put you in jail. You are not her family! Don't forget that.''

''But the money!'' Petey protested. ''We're so close. I know she was going to give me lots of money when we got married. Can't we—''

''Do you want to spend the rest of your life in

prison? I sure don't. I'm out of here. Stay if you want, but I won't.''

He grabbed one of the suitcases she'd gotten out of the closet and began packing. ''It's not fair that we don't get more money. There should be a way to—''

Janelle froze. ''There is,'' she said softly, staring into space. ''At least, there just might be. Hurry!''

JAKE CALLED his mother from his cell phone as he drove Camille and Jamie into Austin. ''Mom? It's Jake. Are you going to be in your office this afternoon?''

''Yes, dear, though I'm going to try to get out of here by four. I want to pick up Chase from the day care and spend some extra time with him. Once Janelle gets the papers, she'll be able to take him home with her. I—I need some time with him.''

''Oh, right. Well, Camille and Jamie are getting their checkups today. We thought we'd drop by and say hello afterward.''

''Oh, wonderful. And you'll bring Jamie with you? I'm dying to see him again. He's such a sweet baby.''

''Yeah, he is, but be sure you speak to us, too, Mom,'' Jake teased.

''Jacob Maitland, quit picking on your mother. Of course I'll say hello to both of you.''

''Good. We'll see you a little after two.''

When he disconnected, Camille was looking at him, a question in her gaze.

''Mom is anxious to see Jamie. I'm not sure she'll

even notice we're in the room once she gets her hands on him. She loves babies.''

Camille didn't seem to have any problem with his mother's attitude. After checking on her baby in the back seat, she said, ''He's adorable, so I can't blame her.''

''And you're not prejudiced at all,'' Jake said with a grin. He couldn't believe it when Camille appeared hurt by his words.

''Hey, I was only teasing. I think Jamie's great.''

''Maybe I am a little partial,'' Camille said, looking sweetly repentant, so much so that Jake wanted to pull the vehicle over and kiss her, ''but he's such a good baby.''

Jake reached over and took her hand in his, threading their fingers. ''Yes, he is. He and I have had some great conversations, too.''

''Oh, you think I get carried away? I'm not pretending he can talk.''

''He's a good listener,'' Jake amended, his smile widening. He loved teasing Camille. He loved her smile. He loved her. All he had to do was convince her. After he caught Eckart.

''Am I going to need to hide when we get to the city?'' she suddenly asked.

''Nope. We've got tinted windows. And Eckart has no way of knowing when we'll show up. We'll be safe. And I talked to Abby earlier, explaining that she needed to see you first. So the checkup won't take long.''

''Good. And you'll keep a close eye on Jamie?''

"Camille, I won't let him out of my sight. I'd never let Vince get his hands on Jamie."

She squeezed his fingers. "I know. I can't tell you how grateful I am that you're protecting us."

He opened his mouth to tell her he loved protecting the two of them, but she held up her hand. "I know, I know. You're going to tell me you're just doing your job. But I'm still grateful."

Those words shut him up. He was doing his job. But he was feeling so much more. Only he'd promised himself he wouldn't say those things until Eckart was in custody. He lifted her palm to his lips, then rested their linked hands on the seat between them.

"We're almost there. After we get out, I want to move quickly. Michael promised to reserve a parking space by the door for us, and he'll try to be there, but the less time you spend outdoors the safer you'll be."

She nodded, saying nothing.

VINCE HATED the gray sedan he was driving. It wasn't new...or fast. But it was bland, unnoticeable. And since he'd been parked in the hospital lot for a couple of days now, that anonymity was important.

When he'd been trying to figure out a way to draw Maitland into town, it had occurred to him that since she'd had a baby, his dear wife would be due for a checkup shortly. Or the baby would. Either way, he'd have his opportunity.

After checking with a local doctor, pretending to be a patient, he'd gotten his answer. Three weeks. He'd figured Camille would come see the doctor sometime this week. He'd already spent Sunday and Monday watching the hospital. He thought they might choose Sunday to trick him, but he was too smart for that.

He wasn't a patient man, though. He wanted to get his son and get out of this hellhole. In the Caribbean, he could live the luxurious life, paid for by his ''earnings,'' instead of sneaking around, living like a street person.

He'd considered leaving the brat behind. It wasn't like he cared about the kid. But he knew taking her son would be the best punishment he could inflict on Camille.

He smiled at the thought of her anguish.

Yeah, that would be worth all the suffering he was having to go through now. And when he was down in the islands, he'd hire someone to take care of the kid. Or have him adopted. He didn't care.

He tossed the can of beer he'd just emptied into the back seat. Reaching into the cooler for another one, he casually checked the driveway. Suddenly, he stiffened. A black Ford Explorer was pulling in.

Maybe he wouldn't have to wait any longer. Maybe he could snatch the kid today. He'd wait until they parked, then move his car next to them. When they came out—

The Explorer didn't park. At least, not in the lot. Instead, it pulled up next to the door in the loading zone. Damn Maitlands! They didn't have to follow any rules.

He watched, his anger building, as Camille slid

from the vehicle, kid in her arms, and hurried inside—out of his reach. Maitland followed, carrying a diaper bag. The wimp! They'd never catch *him* with one of those things.

It occurred to him that he'd have to snatch the bag along with the kid, or his plane trip would be miserable. How did he know what babies needed? Or maybe he'd just kill the kid and then leave. It would save him a lot of trouble. And the thought of Camille's torment was exquisite.

He moved his car into the front row of parking spaces as soon as he saw a spot open up.

He would be ready.

JAKE ESCORTED Camille into Abby's reception area, making sure she was taken in to an examining room at once, before he headed for Morgan's office.

Once there, he and Jamie were shown in immediately, and Morgan joined him. "How's the little guy?"

"He's doing great, aren't you, Jamie?" Jake said.

The nurse took the baby from Jake to weigh him, and Jake hovered over her.

"Relax, Jake," Morgan said with a chuckle. "You're as bad as a first-time dad."

Jake didn't smile. "I *am* a first-time dad. I was there when Jamie was delivered. I've helped care for him since then. He's as much mine as he is Camille's."

Morgan nodded, understanding in his eyes. "Good

for you. I won't worry about this little guy so much if you're going to be looking out for him.''

Jake nodded and watched in silence as Morgan began his examination.

He was almost finished when the door of the examining room burst open. One of Morgan's nurses, her face flushed, said, ''Mr. Maitland, there's an emergency call.''

Jake's first thought was Camille. ''Watch the baby!'' he instructed as he raced from the room.

''Maitland!'' he snapped into the phone the nurse handed him.

''Jake, it's Michael. Chase is gone!''

Jake sagged against the wall. ''What?'' he asked, having difficulty taking in Michael's words. ''What happened? Gone where?''

''Janelle came to pick him up at the day care about noon. She said she wanted to take him for a walk in the park. Your mother had given her permission because she was worried Janelle hasn't been spending enough time with Chase, and he's not going to get used to her.''

''Have you searched the park?''

''Yeah. And the guest house. It's just about empty.''

''Damn! Does Mom know?''

''She's the one who found out Chase was missing. She was going to take him to her office so Camille could see him.''

''I'll be right there, as soon as I pick up Camille.'' He hung up the phone and turned around, only to discover Morgan standing behind him with Jamie in his arms.

"What's wrong?"

"We think Chase has been kidnapped. I've got to go. Are you finished with Jamie? If not, we can—"

"Listen, let me come with you. Chase is Ford Carrington's patient, but Ford's in surgery all afternoon. I want to be available if—if I'm needed." He told the nurse to cancel his remaining appointments.

Jake took Jamie from him and hurried out the door, Morgan on his heels.

Camille was anxiously waiting for him in a locked nurse's office. As soon as she saw Jake's face, she knew something was wrong. Then she saw Morgan, her baby's doctor, with him.

"What's wrong with Jamie?" she asked with a gasp, her hand going to her throat.

"Nothing! He's fine," Jake assured her.

She came out the door, reaching for her baby even as his words registered with her.

"Then why—" she began, her gaze flicking between Jake, Jamie and Morgan.

Jake took her arm and drew her out of the waiting room, trying to minimize the gossip. He whispered, "We think Connor and Janelle have stolen Chase."

"Oh, no!" she said, clutching Jamie more tightly against her chest.

They didn't speak again.

When they reached Megan's office, the reception area was filled with people, most of them family members. Harrison Smith—the real Connor O'Hara—

was among them, and Jake wondered how on earth he'd gotten the news so fast. Megan was distraught, tears streaming down her face.

"But I don't understand. Why would they—the papers were only a formality!"

Jake looked at Michael. "Any word?"

"No." He didn't look happy.

The real Connor stepped forward. "I feel very guilty, Mrs. Maitland. I'm so sorry. What can I do to help?"

His words distracted Megan. "You? Why should you feel guilty?"

The rancher drew a deep breath. "Because—because I'm the real Connor O'Hara. I should have told you sooner."

CHAPTER FIFTEEN

A MUTED UPROAR followed a moment of absolute silence. At first Camille was taken aback by the family's surprise. Then she remembered that they didn't know Smith's true identity.

"What are you saying?" Megan asked in a quavery voice.

"The man you knew as Connor was a con artist," the real Connor explained, his voice gentle but deep with emotion. "I didn't find out about his presence until the night of your party."

"You're Connor? C-Clarise's son?"

"Yes." The real Connor turned to Michael. "Have you confirmed my identity?"

Michael cleared his throat. "We have proof, Megan. This man is the real Connor O'Hara. We were going to tell you this afternoon."

"Is Chase your son?" Megan asked, painful hope in her gaze.

Connor slowly shook his head, sympathy on his face as he reached out and took one of Megan's hands.

Megan Maitland wasn't head of Maitland Maternity Clinic solely because of her name. The courage and strength she was known for were evident as she straightened her shoulders and focused her attention on Michael Lord. "They still took him illegally. Janelle might not be the mother. They must be found."

Megan's barely controlled anguish brought home to Camille how devastated she would be if her ex-husband took Jamie. She'd felt so comfortable, wrapped in Jake's protection, that she'd never actually believed Vince would win.

But Megan hadn't believed anything would happen to Chase, either.

Jake, Michael, Max and Garrett, the foursome who'd gathered around her kitchen table that morning, closed in around Megan. After a brief consultation, Jake came to Camille's side. "We're going back to the cabin. Are you ready?"

"Yes." She didn't hesitate. She felt safe at the cabin. And, in the wake of today's events, she desperately needed to feel safe.

To believe her child was protected.

Within minutes, she and Jamie were strapped into the Explorer, and with Jake at the wheel, they made their way to the safety of the cabin.

VINCE WATCHED a stream of Maitlands pour out of the hospital. What was going on?

He'd observed these people for a few months now. For wealthy people, they were ridiculously hard workers. He'd never seen them take even half a day off.

But putting his curiosity aside, he prepared to follow Maitland and his ex-wife. He wasn't going to lose this opportunity. The last time he'd tried for too much. This time, he only wanted to find their hidey-hole. Then he'd plan his attack.

Half an hour later, he drove slowly past the dirt road that led to a metal gate, proudly announcing the Lord ranch. He didn't follow because he would have been visible to his enemy.

But he'd be back. And this time he'd be successful.

AFTER THEY REACHED the cabin, Camille fed her son and put him to bed. But she lingered by his side, afraid to let him out of her sight.

Suddenly strong arms came around her.

"Is he asleep?" Jake whispered.

She nodded, her throat too tight to speak.

"Come on," Jake said quietly, and began to lead her to her bedroom.

Once he'd closed the door behind the sleeping baby, he turned her to face him and wrapped her in his close embrace. "Scary, isn't it?"

She gulped, fighting to maintain control, and nodded against his chest.

"We're going to protect him, Camille, I promise. I won't let Vince get Jamie."

"But, Jake, your mother would've given anything to protect Chase. She couldn't prevent what happened," she reminded him.

"But I could have. If we'd been honest with Mom before now, she would have taken steps to keep Chase safe."

She heard the agony, the guilt in his voice. Immediately she sought ways to ease his torment. "You couldn't tell her until you had proof. How could she have hidden her feelings around Connor and Janelle? You had no choice, Jake. It's not your fault."

His lips caressed her brow as he stroked her back, holding her even closer. "Sweetheart, I appreciate what you're saying, but I should've done more. I'm a professional, damn it! I should have—"

She pressed her hand to his lips. "Jake, you *are* a professional, one of the most dedicated I know. But you're not Superman."

"I wish I were," he whispered.

Her arms stole around his neck. "You're perfect the way you are. Your mom is so proud of you. She's not going to blame you for what happened. The fault lies with that Petey—and Janelle. Your own cousin! How could she do such a thing?"

Instead of answering, Jake lowered his head and covered her lips with his.

Camille had no objection to this new brand of communication. Even though she'd known, had told herself over and over that there was no future with Jake, she longed for his touch. For the magic of his kiss. And today, when the evil in the world seemed to be closing in on them, she thought she'd die without his arms around her.

"Camille," he whispered, moving his lips from her mouth to her neck.

She arched against him, delighting in his teasing

kisses on her skin, reciprocating with some of her own. "Oh, Jake," she sighed.

His mouth returned to hers, and she drank from him, knowing she'd never get enough of him. His tongue thrust inside her, and she melted.

"Come to bed, sweetheart. Let me love you," he crooned, moving them toward that important piece of furniture.

Camille followed, but her mind wrestled with the decision. She loved this man. Would forever love this man. But they had no future. Was it wise to allow him to love her, knowing he'd soon be out of her life?

But today, with Chase's kidnapping, she'd had to confront the reality of her situation. She had no illusions about what Vince had planned for her, and she couldn't bear to think of Jamie with him. Could she deny herself, and Jake, the one opportunity they had to share the ultimate in love, knowing what they might yet have to face?

No, she couldn't deny him. Or herself.

Her lips eagerly claimed his as he lowered her to the bed, immediately joining her there. He began caressing her body while his lips remained locked on hers, his hands not only touching her, but removing the clothes that intruded. Camille followed his lead, unbuttoning his shirt, reveling in the crisp black hair that covered the muscles of his broad chest.

Jake hooked his thumb in the waistband of her slacks and panties and began easing them down. Camille wanted to urge him to go faster.

Instead, he stopped altogether.

Had he changed his mind? Her heart broke at the thought that she might not have her one chance to love Jake. To discover what true lovemaking was. To erase those times she'd spent with Vince.

"Jake, what's wrong?"

"Sweetheart, is it too soon? I don't want to hurt you. What did Abby say?"

"She said I'm all healed," she hurriedly assured him, moving against him in encouragement. And she wasn't lying, though Abby had suggested she not engage in sexual activity for another few weeks. At the time, she'd assured Abby there was no possibility of that.

She wanted this time with Jake. If it had to last her a lifetime, she still wanted his touch, to be one with him.

"Are you sure?"

Her hands continued to coax him as she nodded. "I'm sure," she whispered.

"I'll be gentle," he promised.

Gentle? She was consumed by fire, by wanting, by a sexual hunger she'd had no idea was in her. Her hands went to the top of his jeans. She didn't want gentle. She wanted Jake. All of him.

His movements grew frantic. She hoped that meant he was being swept away by the magic that enveloped her, too. When they became one, when she felt the power of him inside her, she thought she'd die from the ecstasy. This was more pleasure than she'd known existed.

And it only got better.

Exhausted, they lay still at last, their breathing heavy as they spiraled down from the heights they'd reached. Camille loved the feel of Jake on top of her, her bones like water, her body totally wrapped in his warmth. She couldn't resist touching her lips to his shoulder.

"Sweetheart, are you all right? I didn't hurt you?"

Tears seeped from her eyes, so she buried her face in his neck. "No. Never. You've shown me heaven."

He gathered her closer and slid off her, turning her as he moved, so they faced each other. Without a word, his lips returned to hers in a kiss that was gentle and sweet.

He smiled. "I've never—you were incredible, sweetheart."

Before she could find a way to tell him how much their lovemaking had meant to her, the phone rang.

They both tensed. It seemed incredible, after the ecstasy they'd shared, that the world could intrude.

Jake kissed her again. "Stay here and rest," he said, and slipped from the bed.

Camille turned her head to watch his powerful, naked body as he hurried out of her room. He was a magnificent man, inside as well as outside. Gratitude filled her that, no matter what else happened, they'd shared this time together.

"HELLO?" Jake answered the phone, irritation in his voice.

"Bad timing?" Garrett asked.

"You could say that," Jake drawled, his mind on Camille nestled in her bed, her honey-soft skin urging his touch.

"Sorry about that. But your mother has been talking to your partner, Greg, about the kidnapping. So far, there's been no trace of them. Needless to say, Megan is anxious. We thought we'd have a strategy meeting this evening and we want you to be there."

Jake couldn't say no. But much as he loved his mother, he wanted to. He wanted to stay here with Camille and Jamie and hold the world at bay. And he definitely wasn't going to leave them alone.

"You'll have to have the meeting here. I can't leave Camille and the baby alone. Today's events shook her up. With good reason."

"But if she hears us tonight, she might get upset even more."

"I can't leave her alone, Garrett. You know that. If you want me at the meeting, it'll be here. Or you can do without me." He wanted to help. But Camille and Jamie needed him.

"Okay, okay. We'll be there about eight. I'll get the latest news from Greg before we come."

Jake hung up the phone and immediately returned to Camille's bedroom, eager to hold her close again. Even as he thought of doing so, his body seconded the motion. Damn, he hoped she wasn't too sore. He couldn't believe he wanted her again so soon. But in his heart, he acknowledged that he would always want her. More and more. Loving her hadn't assuaged his hunger. It had increased it. A first for him.

He pushed open the door to her room, his heart leaping eagerly, anxious to see her again. But she'd pulled the sheet over her naked body. And she was asleep.

Fighting the desire to awaken her, he stared at her. He couldn't be so cruel. She'd had a difficult day and needed her rest.

The desire to protect her, to do what was best for her, overrode the hunger he felt. He loved her. He would let her rest. For now.

Backing out of the room, he closed the door quietly. Then he checked on Jamie before he settled down to think out a plan to trap Janelle and her partner, Petey.

And to find a way to bring the saga with Vince Eckart to a close.

WHEN JAMIE awakened Camille several hours later, she responded at once, her mind still fogged with sleep. By the time she'd changed him and lifted him from his bed, she realized she felt better than she had in months. But she was a little sore.

Then she remembered why.

Settling into the rocker in her bedroom, she realized she felt a mixture of ecstasy and despair. She loved Jake. What they'd shared was more powerful, more moving than she'd ever thought intimacy could be. But she'd have to learn to live without that experience for the rest of her life.

When Vince was caught, Jake would set her free. Oh, he'd be kind. But she didn't fit in to his life.

scent. The slight indentation showed her where his head had rested after their lovemaking, when he'd held her tenderly in his arms.

Abruptly, she leaped from the bed, hoping to escape those memories.

In the same instant a popping sound sent an eerie chill through her, and the glass in her window exploded.

Oh, God, she thought, instinctively throwing herself to the floor. Vince had found her.

CHAPTER SIXTEEN

JAKE'S HEART almost stopped.

He knew the sound, had heard it often enough. Before anyone else at the table had moved, he was charging down the hall, bellowing Camille's name.

When he reached her room, he found her on the floor beside the bed. Immediately he killed the lights as another shot hit the wall beside him. Then he fell to the floor and gathered her into his arms, his hands frantically traveling down her body to find any injury.

"Jake," she whispered. "Is it Vince?"

"Yeah, probably. Are you hurt? Did you take the first bullet?"

"No," she said, her voice stressed. "I moved suddenly and—and the bullet hit my pillow."

"Is she all right?" Garret called, stepping into the doorway.

"Get down. Kill the hall light," Jake ordered harshly.

Both orders were promptly followed. Then Garrett asked again, his voice soft. "Is she all right?"

"Yeah."

"Jamie!" Camille said with a gasp, her shock wearing off.

"I'll get the baby," Jake said, his voice leaving no room for argument. "Guys, take her into the kitchen, but turn off the lights before you enter."

Camille didn't want to go with the others. She wanted to keep her eyes fixed on Jake, to know that he was safe. To know that he would save Jamie.

But when Jake had taken on the job of protecting them, she'd given her solemn oath to do as he asked, whenever, whatever.

She couldn't hold back a plea. "Jake, be careful. The night-light—"

His lips covered hers in a hard kiss, a determined kiss. "I know," he assured her when he lifted his head. Then he left her and crawled to the connecting door and Jamie.

Once Jake made it to the kitchen, Jamie in his arms, he handed him to Camille. Then he opened the kitchen drawer where he'd placed his gun.

"It appears Vince is alone. All the bullets came through Camille's room. I'm going to—"

Another shot interrupted him, this one shattering the living room window.

"Looks like I'm going to owe you some new glass in the morning," he muttered to Garrett. Then he continued with the plan he'd come up with while fetching Jamie. "I'm going to sneak out the back door and find him."

"No!" Camille gasped. "No, Jake. He hates you. He'll kill you without any hesitation. Stay here, stay safe." She gulped. "I—I can't be responsible for you being hurt."

Max, his voice calm but low, agreed. "She's right, Jake. I'll slip out. You stay here. Camille needs you."

"No!" Jake replied sharply. "This is an FBI case. I'm in charge. I'm going out."

"I'm going with you," Max said calmly, as if he were discussing a stroll in the park.

Michael and Garrett volunteered, too.

"Look," Jake said. "Somebody's got to guard Camille and Jamie."

Michael put his hand on Jake's shoulder. "I'll stay."

Jake nodded, then turned to Camille. "I want you and the baby on the floor here where the cabinets form a V. You'll be safe in the dark with Michael." Then he gave her a hard kiss and led the three other men out the door into the night.

"Oh, God, please...please keep them safe," Camille pleaded in a whisper as she slid to the floor. She couldn't bear it if any of them were killed... especially Jake.

In the dark, she cuddled Jamie tightly against her chest, trying to see through the black night. There was no moon tonight, and every sound seemed to echo in the darkness. She tried to breathe more quietly. Jamie squeaked, and Camille loosened her hold and began rocking back and forth on the floor. The familiar movement made her feel better. Until she heard a spate of gunfire. She covered her mouth with one hand to keep a moan from escaping.

Michael tensed beside her, and she could sense him tightening his grip on his gun. Camille couldn't bear just sitting there, not knowing if Jake was dead or alive.

She reached out and clutched Michael's arm. "Go," she ordered him in desperation. "Go check on Jake or I swear to you, I will."

When Michael started to protest, she tightened her hold.

"I mean it, Michael. Go now—out the back door—then come and tell me what's happened. What if Vince has killed them all?" Her voice wavered at the thought, but she fought for control. "You and I will have to get out of here somehow. Go—*please!*"

"Okay, Camille, I'll go. But promise me you'll stay here till I get back."

"Just go," Camille cried, close to hysteria.

Silently Michael rose and made his way down the hallway, soundless in the darkened cabin.

"Please, please, please," Camille whispered. In the deserted kitchen, her voice sounded amplified. She desperately strained to see anything. But she could make out nothing.

She kissed Jamie's forehead and leaned back against the cabinets, her eyes closed.

They shot open when the light in the kitchen went on. There before her loomed her worst nightmare. Vincent Eckart pointed his gun at her and Jamie, an evil grin on his face.

"Well, well, well, my little wife, it's about time I caught up with you."

"What did you do to the others?" she asked, her voice trembling.

His grin widened. "What do you think I did to them?"

Camille fought the tears as she held Jamie close.

"Is that the brat? Did you name him after me?"

Anger chased the tears away. "I wouldn't name a cockroach after you, Vince!"

"Just for that remark, my dear, I think I'll kill the kid first, so you can watch him die."

"No!" she screamed, curling around the baby, trying to turn her back on the devil in front of her.

He lined her up in the gun's sights. "Oh, yes, dear Camille. Oh, yes,"

The pleasure in his words was pure evil. He would kill his own child and enjoy it.

"Drop it, Eckart," Jake ordered, rushing through the door, his arms extended, his gun in his hands.

Camille stared, relief flooding her. Until Vince swung his gun toward Jake.

"You drop it, or I'll kill my dear wife."

Camille knew she would probably die, but she didn't want her baby or Jake to suffer. "Vince! Vince, I'll go with you, do whatever, if you'll let Jamie and Jake live." She clamped her mouth shut to keep the sobs inside her.

His gun swung toward her. "No, babe. I don't want you anymore...except dead."

As if he were moving in slow motion, Camille saw his finger tighten on the gun. When she heard the sound of gunfire, she tensed for the pain. For death.

Instead, Vince crumpled to the floor, a stunned look on his face.

She watched in shock as Jake crossed to Vince's body and checked for a pulse.

"Is...is he dead?" Her voice cracked. She was ashamed at the relief that filled her when Jake nodded. Her ex-husband was dead. And she was glad.

"Jake, the others? Are they all right?"

Before Jake answered, she heard sirens in the distance.

OVER AND OVER, Camille blamed herself for Garrett's pain. The ambulance had finally arrived. The medics had stopped the blood flow, started an IV and loaded him in the ambulance.

The others headed for Garrett's truck to follow.

Jake came to her. Camille was ready. She'd grabbed Jamie's diaper bag. She wasn't going to be left behind.

"You're safe," Jake assured her. "Vince is dead. No one will hurt you now, but I'm going to have one of the agents stay with you."

"I'm going with you."

"Sweetheart, I don't know when we'll get back. It could be late."

She stepped around him and headed for the door. "I'm going with you," she repeated over her shoulder. She knew he could physically force her to stay, but she didn't think he would.

They raced through the night in Jake's Explorer, neither speaking. Michael and Max, in Garrett's truck, followed close behind.

Fortunately, Garrett was the only one shot, other

than Vince, but his condition was extremely serious. He'd lost a lot of blood.

When they reached Austin's main hospital, they parked in the driveway and rushed in behind the paramedics. The ambulance had transported Vince's body, also, and as soon as the medics turned Garrett over to the doctors, they returned to bring in the body. As they passed Camille, she asked them to stop. She had to see for herself that the man who had made her life a living hell was truly dead.

Call it gruesome or insensitive or even crazy, she had to see him one last time. Pulling the sheet back, she stared at her ex-husband. His expression was stunned, as if he couldn't believe he'd lost. He'd always thought he was invincible.

Jake's arm came around her, offering support.

The paramedic looked at her. "Can you identify him, ma'am?"

She tried to speak, but Jake took over. "We both can. He was wanted by the FBI. His name is Vincent Eckart."

He pulled out his badge and showed it to the man.

"I'll make a note of that, sir," the paramedic assured him.

Jake leaned down to whisper in Camille's ear. "Stay here with Michael and Max. I've got to talk to Greg, then call Mom." He slipped away.

Camille held her baby against her, her eyes shut. The guilt that filled her only worsened as she thought of Megan Maitland. She was such a strong, giving woman. But how much could she take?

Chase had been kidnapped by a man who had betrayed Megan's trust and her freely given love. Now Garrett had been shot. Camille knew Megan loved the Lord siblings almost as much as her own children.

She would never forgive Camille for putting him in danger.

Jake returned and slipped his arm around her again.

"Did you talk to your mother?" she asked softly.

"Yeah. She's on her way. Abby's going to bring her. She'll be able to get some answers. Shelby's coming with them, and Lana will come later."

Max stood and began pacing the floor.

"Did you talk to Greg?" Camille asked, worried that Jake might face charges for killing Vince.

"Yeah," Jake said calmly.

"What did he say?"

"Not much. I gave him my gun and badge."

"Oh, Jake!" Camille said with a gasp.

"It's standard procedure, sweetheart. I told you there's nothing to worry about."

Guilt deepened in Camille. She'd put Jake's entire family in danger, and Garrett lay in critical condition in the hospital because of her mistakes. Because of her ex-husband. And now she'd endangered his career.

She hung her head, trying to hide the tears.

Megan and Abby, followed by Shelby, erupted into the emergency waiting room. Questions poured forth. Jake didn't have any answers and asked Abby to see what she could find out.

As Abby went to speak to the doctors, Greg waved

for Jake to join him and several newcomers. Squeezing Camille's hand, he left her and walked over to them. The men huddled together, leaving Shelby and Megan with Camille.

"I'm—I'm so sorry." She managed to get out the words, fighting off the tears.

Megan reached over to hold Camille's free hand. "Darling, it's not your fault. All the blame goes to that evil man."

"But I brought him into your lives!" Camille protested, her voice rising. She heard the note of hysteria and clamped down on her emotions. She didn't want to make the waiting more difficult than it already was.

"How did Garrett—" Shelby began, then paused to control her wavering voice. "I mean, Jake and Michael were there. Garrett's a rancher, not—"

It was a difficult answer to give, one that condemned Camille again, but she felt she had to answer it. "Vince—Vince started shooting while they were having their meeting. Jake was going to go outside, to face Vince, and—and the others decided to go with him. Garrett got shot. I'm so sorry. I—I wish—"

Megan reached out and clasped Camille's hand. "We all do, darling. We all do."

Shelby took Megan's other hand, and the three women sat waiting.

ABBY RETURNED a few minutes later to report that Garrett was stabilized. He'd lost a lot of blood, but the bullet had entered his left shoulder, above the heart, and hadn't done too much damage.

"Can we see him?" Megan asked.

"Two at a time. You and Shelby, Michael and Jake," Abby explained. "I don't think he'll be up to much more."

WHILE MEGAN and Shelby went in Garrett's room, Jake came back to Camille's side. He asked Max, standing nearby, if he could borrow his cell phone. He'd been bothered by the fact that Vince had found them. Even if he'd tailed them to the ranch, he wouldn't have known about the cabin.

He dialed the number to the ranch. "Mrs. Easley, did anyone come to the ranch this evening?"

"Why, yes, Mr. Maitland. Your friend in the FBI. He said he was supposed to be meeting with you, and Mr. Lord told him to stop at the house for directions."

"He told you he was FBI?" Jake asked sharply.

"And he showed me his badge. Mr. Parks, I believe he was."

"I see. Thanks. Oh, Mrs. Easley, Garrett had a little accident and he'll be at the hospital for a couple of days. We'll let you know when he's coming home."

"Oh, dear Lord," Mrs. Easley cried. "I thought I heard sirens, but I turned in early tonight and figured I was dreaming. What on earth happened?"

Jake briefly answered her concerned questions, then hung up the phone and handed it back to Max. Greg came over. Before he could speak, Jake said, "Eckart stole Steve's badge and ID. He used them to get info from Garrett's housekeeper. You'd better check his belongings."

"Damn. I didn't think to look for those when Steve was killed." Greg frowned. "I guess I'm partly to blame for this entire fiasco."

"There's plenty of blame to go around," Jake said, "but ultimately it belongs to me. Eckart was my responsibility." He rubbed the back of his neck. "As long as Garrett recovers, things won't be so bad. But I was afraid—"

"We all were," Max assured him, patting him on the shoulder.

"Do you want to go in to see him?" Jake asked. "Abby said two more could go in. Michael, of course, but—"

"You go. I'll see him tomorrow. Or later tonight."

Jake thanked him just as Megan and Shelby emerged, visibly upset.

Jake hurried over. "Has he taken a turn for the worse?" he asked anxiously.

"No, no, he's doing much better," Megan assured him, wiping her eyes. "He's even complaining, which is a good sign, but he's—he's so pale."

Shelby spoke. "I'm going to stay with him tonight. Probably when Lana gets here, she'll stay, too. They're moving him upstairs to a real room, one of those private ones with a sofa."

"I'll stay," Michael protested.

"No, you need to help find Chase," Shelby reminded him. "Megan's counting on you."

"But—" Michael began, then stopped and nodded. "You're right."

Abby signaled for the next pair to come, and Michael and Jake entered the small examining room.

MEGAN TURNED to Camille. "I understand the cabin was shot up pretty badly. I want you and the baby to come to my house for the night. We—we have that big nursery where Jamie will be just fine."

Camille squeezed her eyes shut, then opened them. "Mrs. Maitland, that's more than generous, considering how responsible I am for Garrett's condition. I couldn't take advantage of you. When Jake is free, I'll get him to take us back to the cabin. We'll be fine there."

"We'll see what Jake says. He may not be free for a while. There's always a lot of paperwork involved when someone is killed."

Camille sat in tense silence waiting for Jake's return. What would he say? She wanted him to come with her, to hold her, but she knew better.

It was over.

Vince was dead, and there was no threat to her or Jamie any longer. It had ended sooner than she'd expected. She'd hoped for at least one more time in Jake's arms. One more night of loving to treasure for the rest of her life.

Jake and Michael came out. Max met them, anxious for news of Garrett.

"He's tired, drained, but he's doing fine," Jake assured Max. "He said to say thanks for saving his bacon."

Max dismissed such thanks as unnecessary, but

Camille had learned that he'd shielded Garrett's body with his while firing at Vince after Garrett had been hit.

Megan wrapped her arms around Max and hugged him. "Garrett is right to thank you. You protected him and got him help, and that's the only reason he's alive. I owe you any favor you want."

Max turned bright red and looked to Jake for help.

"Okay, Mom," Jake said, putting his arm around his mother, "you're embarrassing him. Listen, can you take Camille home with you? I'm going to the office with Greg and try to wrap things up. I don't want her going back to the cabin."

Camille rose out of the chair she'd occupied since they'd arrived. "No, Jake, you can't ask that of your mother."

Surprised, Jake stared at her. "Why not?"

"Jake, this was all my fault. Your mother shouldn't have to—I mean, it must be painful to her to even be in the same room with me...." Camille could barely finish the sentence.

Jake left his mother's side and caught Camille's shoulders. "No one blames you, sweetheart. And I can't get my job done unless I know you're okay. I don't know when I'll get in, so I'll see you tomorrow. You have everything you need for Jamie?"

She nodded, realizing she had no choice. "But doesn't Greg want to talk to me?"

Jake surprised her by delivering another of those hard kisses, brief but memorable, then he ducked his head and kissed Jamie's forehead.

"Not tonight. If he does later, it will just be a formality." Without saying anything else, he kissed his mother's cheek and hurried to Greg, who was waiting by the door to the hospital emergency room.

CAMILLE DIDN'T get a lot of sleep that night. Her room was lovely and located right next door to the nursery. Jamie awakened her several times, seemingly when she'd been asleep only a few minutes.

The rest of the time, she tried to think about her future. She needed to plan her life. A life she would live without Jake.

After feeding Jamie early the next morning, she repacked his diaper bag, wrapped the receiving blanket around him and tiptoed down the main staircase. She'd driven Jake's Explorer from the hospital to Megan's house the night before. She intended to use his vehicle to go to the cabin and pack. Then she'd drive it to the airport and call Megan to tell her where Jake could find it.

She couldn't face him to say goodbye. She'd write a note explaining how grateful she was. But her emotions were too strung out to look him in the eye and say goodbye.

She just couldn't.

Megan came out of the dining room as she reached the bottom of the stairs.

"Camille, I hoped you'd get to sleep longer. But Jamie woke you, of course. Did you get much rest last night?"

"Yes, thank you, Mrs. Maitland. And thank you

for your hospitality," she added, edging toward the door.

Megan slipped her arm under Camille's. "We're delighted to have you here. Now, come to breakfast. You must keep up your strength so that little boy gets plenty to eat."

She sounded so much like Jake, Camille was led willy-nilly into the dining room before she could come up with a reason to escape.

Even as Megan seated her next to the chair at the end of the table, the one she'd occupied the night of the party, Camille gave it a try. "I really don't eat breakfast, but thank you—"

"Child, you must take better care of yourself." She summoned her butler. "Now, what would you like? My kitchen can prepare almost anything. An omelette? Pancakes? That was always Jake's favorite. Fortunately, it never seems to go to fat. He's in magnificent condition."

Camille's cheeks turned bright red. She knew. She'd seen him naked, stroked his muscular body, felt his strength. "Uh, really, I don't—"

Megan ignored her. "Bring some fruit, buttered toast and bacon for both of us." After the butler had left the room, she added, "You'll need the protein."

Camille stared at her. Jamie stirred against her, and Megan held out her arms. "May I hold him? Just for a minute? I—I miss Chase so much."

After that appeal, Camille couldn't say no.

An hour later, she finally escaped Megan's mothering. What a wonderful woman. When Jake married, his wife would have a wonderful mother-in-law, a great family.

Which only highlighted her loneliness.

She pressed down on the accelerator, anxious to escape before she fell to her knees to plead with Jake not to let her go.

CHAPTER SEVENTEEN

JAKE DROVE carefully to his mother's. He hadn't gotten much sleep last night. He didn't want to have an accident now. Not when things were finally going his way.

Vincent Eckart was dead.

Jake had tied up all the loose ends, then he'd talked with his superior in D.C. He'd asked for leave and warned the man he was thinking of quitting the Company. The man's protests were flattering, but Jake knew his decision was the right one.

And now he was going to finalize the most important decision in his life. Whatever he chose to do, he wanted to do it with Camille and Jamie at his side.

He checked the time as he pulled into his mother's driveway. Almost two o'clock. He hadn't planned to be gone so long, but there'd been a lot to do. And he'd slept a few hours in Greg's office.

Harold, the butler, greeted him as he came in.

"Where's Mrs. Eckart?" he asked. He couldn't wait until Camille no longer answered to that name.

"She's gone, Mr. Jake," Harold said.

"Gone? Gone where?"

"I don't know. Mrs. Maitland spoke with her. Perhaps she—"

"Mom!" Jake roared, charging forward.

Megan stepped into the long entryway, having been in her private sitting room. "Jake, you're back. Is everything all right? I called the hospital, and Garrett is doing much better."

"Yeah. Where's Camille?"

"She took your car and went back to the cabin. I couldn't convince her to stay." Megan frowned. "She seemed quite determined to go."

Jake panicked. Suddenly he knew. She was going to leave. He grabbed the phone in the butler's pantry and dialed the number at the cabin. His heart almost stopped beating as he waited for each long, excruciating ring. No answer.

He slammed down the receiver. "If you hear from her, you tell her to get back here. Tell her I'll come after her if she doesn't."

Alarm flashed across Megan's face, but Jake didn't bother to reassure her. He didn't have time. He didn't have the words, because he didn't know how to reassure himself.

Damn it! They'd made love. She couldn't just walk out of his life as if it hadn't mattered. She'd wanted him as much as he'd wanted her. It was impossible—

He crawled behind the wheel of his government-issued car and slammed his foot on the accelerator. There was an urgency filling him that told him he didn't have a minute to spare.

CAMILLE KNEW she had to hurry. She shouldn't even be here. The cabin was surrounded by yellow police tape, but the one officer who'd been there when she'd arrived had said she could go in, as long as she stayed outside the taped-off areas.

Now even he had left, and apparently the media had taken all the photos they'd wanted, too. She and Jamie were completely alone.

She stared at the piece of paper in front of her. She'd left this chore for last. Their personal belongings were packed, and Jamie was fed, so he'd be content for a few hours. She'd even loaded everything in the Ford Explorer.

Then she'd written a note to Garrett and one to Megan Maitland.

Now she had to write Jake.

But what could she say? Thank you for teaching me how wonderful love can be? Thank you for risking your life to protect us? Thank you for…for being Jake Maitland, the most wonderful man in the world?

She was determined not to sound like a whiner, a woman who wanted more than he could give. He owed her nothing. He'd done his best for her, and what had she given him in return? She'd endangered both him and his family and had indirectly almost caused the death of his good friend Garrett.

She'd called this morning to make sure Garrett was progressing. They'd offered to let her talk to him, but she'd refused.

With a heavy sigh, she picked up the pen and got as far as "Dear Jake." She sighed again, then looked at her watch. She'd gotten plane reservations for her and Jamie at four o'clock. She'd need to leave soon.

Suddenly she seized the pen and wrote a polite thank-you. She didn't know what else to say. A thank-you was hardly enough for all Jake had done, but it was the best she could manage.

She'd almost finished when the sound of an approaching vehicle interrupted her. She leaped to her feet and ran to the kitchen window.

A nondescript gray sedan was traveling too fast for the dirt road, sending up a plume of dust behind it. She didn't know anyone who drove that kind of car. Uneasiness filled her. She had no weapon. Vince might be gone, but maybe he had associates who would—

The car skidded to a halt, stirring up dust and making it impossible to see the occupant...until he got out.

Jake.

Camille drew a deep breath, but she was shaking. This was one interview she'd tried to avoid. She stepped back from the door, instinctively knowing from Jake's angry stride that she didn't want to be close to him now.

"Why the hell didn't you answer the phone?" he demanded as he stormed into the kitchen.

She shrugged and tried for a casual air, sure she was failing miserably. "Only your mother knew where I was, and I'd just left her. I thought it would be for you."

His gaze trained on her, Jake took a step closer, making her nervous. "And you were too busy packing, right?"

She sucked in air. He knew she was leaving. "Y-yes. I have to hurry. My plane leaves—"

"No, it doesn't." His flat statement confounded her.

"Yes, it leaves at four, Jake. I was going to park your car at the airport so you could retrieve it, but—"

"I canceled your reservation."

Those words stopped her. "You did what?"

"You're not going anywhere, Camille. At least, not until we've talked about a few things." His voice was hard, unyielding.

He'd been that way in the beginning, shielding himself from her friendliness. She drew a deep breath. It was better this way. She could remain strong as long as his gentle side was hidden from her.

"I wrote you a—" She began to explain, hoping to escape that talk he wanted to have.

He looked behind her and crossed the kitchen to snatch the paper off the table.

She watched warily as he scanned the pitifully few words she'd managed to put down.

"Thank you? *Thank you?*" he repeated, his voice rising. "That's all you have to say about what happened between us?"

"Jake, I understand that you didn't intend—we'd spent so much time together that it was—I didn't expect a commitment. I know how inappropriate any— I don't fit in. And I caused Garrett's injury. I wouldn't blame you and your entire family if you hoped you'd never see me again."

JAKE STARED AT HER, her fragile beauty more tempting than ever. "What do you mean, you don't fit in?"

A desperate look filled her eyes. He didn't know if it was because she wanted to escape him, or because she found his question difficult to answer. *He* certainly couldn't imagine why she'd said such a thing.

Exasperation laced her words. "Jake, I've never been in such an elegant house as your mother's. I've never worn a designer dress, been to a formal party. I'm strictly middle-class." She paused, and before Jake could speak, added, "And I was married to Vince."

Jake stepped close enough to pull her into his arms. He couldn't wait any longer to touch her. "Vince is dead. But you didn't wait for his death to free yourself. You took care of that all by yourself when you filed for divorce." His mouth covered hers briefly. He raised his head and stared at her, looking for an objection to his caress. There wasn't any, which gave him hope.

"Second, I left home because my fiancée was counting the money and the social ties she would receive when she married me. She would've married a jackrabbit if he'd offered her the same. I decided I didn't want a woman who loved things more than me."

"Jake—"

He kissed her again. Longer, deeper, and found it more difficult to lift his head.

"Knowing you," he continued, "you're blaming

yourself for Garrett getting hurt. But it wasn't your fault, and he's raising hell today with all the nurses."

He'd given her time to protest that last kiss. To push him away. To tell him his touch bothered her. She hadn't done any of those things. Encouraged, he pulled her even tighter against him, pressing her warmth to him, feeling her heart race along with his.

"Most important," he finished, his voice dropping to a whisper, "I love you. I love Jamie. I want you both in my life for as long as we live. I want to be your protector forever."

"Jake!" Camille cried, wrapping her arms around his neck and burying her face against his chest. "Jake, you can't," she protested.

He pulled back to see her face. Then he kissed her again. This time it took several minutes for him to release her lips. Several minutes while he debated whether to pick her up and seek out the nearest bed.

But he wanted all the talking done before he pleasured both of them. He wanted commitment, not just a roll in the hay. "Why can't I?"

"Your mother—all your family must hate me. They wouldn't accept—"

"Is that your only objection?"

"I don't want you to feel…obligated because we made love," she whispered, her eyes filling with tears.

Jake laughed, shaking his head. "Lord have mercy, sweetheart. Obligated? Do I feel obligated to you?" he asked, pressing himself against her.

"Men—men like sex," she said breathlessly, her cheeks bright red.

"You bet I do. And I hope you do, too. Because I plan to share a bed with you for the rest of my life. Let's try this again. I love you. I love Jamie. I want us to marry, to legally be a family."

"Jake—"

"You're messing up your role. You're supposed to say you love me, too."

"Of course I love you," she confessed with a sob. "Enough that I want you to be happy. To be with your family. Not to be ostracized because you married a gangster's wife and are raising his son."

He rewarded her words with a kiss that almost had him undressing her right there on the kitchen floor. But first things first. Breathing heavily, he said, "We're already a family. I consider Jamie to be my son. After all, he's named after me. All I want is to make it legal."

"Oh, Jake, I want that, too, but I don't think you understand. Your family—"

"I love my family. And I want to stay here, in Texas. I want to raise Jamie with all the cousins who are sure to come along. But you and Jamie are my family, too. The most important members of it. You're underestimating Mom and the others. They all admire you—some a little too much," he added darkly, remembering the men's reaction to her appearance in her designer dress. "They'll shoot me if I let you get away." He drew a deep breath, but he didn't dare kiss her again. Not yet. Because if he did, there wouldn't be any more talk. Not for several hours.

"They always say third time's the charm. Will you marry me, Camille? Will you let me adopt Jamie, be his father?"

He held his breath, hoping and praying she'd say what he wanted to hear.

With a sob, she nodded. His lips seized hers, and they celebrated their commitment in a searing kiss. Swinging her into his arms, he started down the hall.

Then they heard another car approaching.

"Damn it!" Jake exclaimed. He didn't want to wait to take Camille to bed so he could show her how much he loved her. He'd deal with whoever it was quickly. Setting Camille down, he turned to the kitchen.

She followed.

An attractive woman got out of a car and started toward the door.

Camille's arm slid around Jake's waist. "If this is your old girlfriend coming back to stake a claim, I'm going to fight her."

Jake grinned at her. "I'll help you, 'cause I'm not interested in anyone but you. Unfortunately, I know this woman and she's wanting information, not me."

"Who is she?"

"Chelsea Markum, that talk show reporter who deals in gossip." Even as Jake swung open the door, he heard another car approaching. Had the cabin suddenly turned into Grand Central Station?

"What do you want?" he asked, shielding Camille from the woman.

"I want to do a story on the woman you've been keeping in hiding—Vince Eckart's ex-wife. I want—"

A familiar truck screeched to a halt, and Max sprang out. "What are you doing here?" he yelled, his stride furious and quick.

"I'm a legitimate reporter," she protested, backing up. "And I have a right to be here. I got the information from the paper this morning. and I asked the housekeeper's permission."

Camille saw for the first time that she had a camcorder in her hands.

"Like hell you did," Max returned.

Jake interrupted. "Look, this isn't a good time for an interview. I'd like you to leave the property."

"You can't throw me off. I haven't done anything wrong." The woman lifted her chin and stubbornly stared at him.

Max took her arm. "I'll get rid of her, Jake. You go back to whatever you're doing."

"Thanks, Max. I owe you one."

Jake was swinging the door closed when the woman screamed and something crashed. Camille pushed past Jake to see Max carrying the beautiful young woman over his shoulder, fireman-style, toward his truck.

"Jake, I don't think Max should—I mean, she'll probably sue him. And she dropped her camera. What if it's broken?"

Jake shrugged and firmly closed the door. "Max will manage. I trust him. Don't you?"

"Yes, yes, I do." As she heard the roar of Max's truck as it left the cabin, she realized there wasn't anything she could do, anyway. She certainly couldn't call the cops, not after Max had helped her so much.

"Good. Then I want you to concentrate on me, Mrs. Soon-to-be Maitland, not on that gossipmonger in Max's truck. We've got more important things to do than that."

With her arms around his neck, she kissed him, a kiss that drove any kind of thought from his head. By the time they reached the bed, he had half her clothes off her.

"Oh, Jake," Camille said with a sigh that only intensified his hunger. "I feel so guilty being this happy when Garrett is in the hospital and Chase is missing."

"We're going to do what we can to find Chase, sweetheart, and Garrett is recovering," Jake said. "But right now, I have to concentrate on convincing you that I love you."

"I'm convinced," she drawled, a beautiful smile on her lips, "but don't let that stop you."

He didn't.

EPILOGUE

THREE DAYS LATER, Camille and Jake, with Jamie, returned to Megan's luxurious home. Jake had spent that time convincing Camille they were perfect for each other.

While she'd enjoyed the convincing more than she'd ever thought possible, she was still concerned about his family's reaction. "Jake, did you tell your mother—"

"That we were sleeping together?" he asked, a grin on his lips.

"No! Of course you wouldn't—Jake Maitland, stop teasing me!"

"But you look so cute when you turn all red," he said, still smiling.

She gave him a stern look. "Did you tell your mother I'm still here?"

"Of course I did. I also told her I loved you and that I'm going to marry you and adopt Jamie."

"When did you do that? I didn't hear that conversation."

"Well, no, because I'd exhausted you in bed," he assured her, puffing out his chest with pride. "I'm a real stud."

She shook her head, smiling at his teasing, but she could hardly disagree with him. "What—what did your mother say?"

"She said congratulations, she couldn't be happier. And she is thrilled to have another baby in the family."

"I feel so badly for her," Camille said. "Isn't there any word on Chase yet?"

"Not yet." For the first time, Jake sounded grim.

"It's so generous of your mother to allow the wedding to go on when she's so upset."

"Anna had it all planned. They'd already switched the date once and were going to lose the money they'd paid for Janelle's wedding. When Mom suggested Morgan and Mary Jane be the happy couple, they agreed."

"Your mother is an incredible woman."

"Yeah, she is. You remind me of her. And, by the way, she suggested we should be the ones getting married today."

An hour later, Camille watched the newlyweds walk down the aisle, their vows exchanged. She couldn't stop the tears in her eyes.

"Hey, you okay?" Jake asked solicitously.

"Yes," she said, leaning against his strong shoulder. "I'm so happy for them."

"I'll be happier when it's our turn."

She'd asked him to wait, to give his family time to express their feelings about his marrying her. She wanted to be sure their marriage wouldn't cause problems.

Now she regretted her decision.

"I wish it had been us today, too," she whispered.

He kissed her, in front of everyone, and whispered in her ear, "Soon."

"Break it up, you two," Garrett said. He'd sat beside Jake during the wedding.

"You're just jealous," Jake said, casually taking Garrett's arm to support him as they walked over to the reception area.

"You're right," Garrett agreed, smiling. "I'm feeling a little lonely with everyone around me getting married. Pretty soon we'll need name tags to know who everyone is."

Camille smiled at him. "I doubt that. I've never seen such a loving family. You welcome newcomers so warmly."

"None more than you, sweetheart," Jake said, squeezing her. "Especially because Mom gets a new grandchild. You know how she loves babies."

Camille smiled in agreement, but she knew Megan loved each and every one of her children, including the Lords. But she'd never be completely happy until Chase was found. Camille crossed her fingers, hoping for a happy ending for Megan, as happy as the end of her own crisis had been.

Or maybe she should call it a great beginning rather than a happy end. She and Jake, with Jamie, had a wonderful future. She hoped that would happen for all the Maitlands. They deserved it.

MAITLAND MATERNITY
continues with
THE TODDLER'S TALE
by
Rebecca Winters

*P.I. Max Jamison had had enough of
Tattle Today TV reporter Chelsea Markum
and her poison pen. He was telling her just
that when an unexpected crisis
stopped him cold. A small child's life
depended on him and Chelsea working
together, in spite of their
volatile relationship....*

*Available next month
Here's a preview!*

CHAPTER ONE

WITHOUT WARNING, Max stood on the brakes. His action killed the motor. *Wonderful!* Chelsea thought. They were out in the middle of nowhere.

When he turned his powerful physique toward her, she noticed a muscle twitching at one corner of his jaw. His handsome features had hardened into a grim facsimile of the flesh-and-blood man who made her pulse race faster than she deemed healthy.

She struggled for composure under the fierce accusation of eyes more black than brown in the semi-dark interior of the truck.

"You call it responsible reporting when you trespass on the Lord ranch, interfere with police and FBI business, cause grief to everyone, just so you could get some damn photos of Camille and her baby?

"Dare I hope that one day you'll be a victim of someone like yourself? It could be an enlightening experience."

Though they'd skirmished many times in the past, Max had never yelled at her to make a point. Another trait she grudgingly respected in Max Jamison. Well-chosen words, not noise, were his scalpel. Like a great surgeon, he knew precisely where to cut, how deep to penetrate to get at that hidden core of suffering inside her.

Willing tears not to form, Chelsea averted her eyes. ''Don't you know *anything* is possible in this worl—''

He cut her off without preamble. *''What's that?''* In an abrupt move, he shifted in his seat, turning away from her. ''Listen! There it is again. Do you hear it?''

Chelsea assumed he'd heard the wind, which had been buffeting the truck, but she rolled down her window all the same. Gust-driven raindrops pelted her face.

She shivered from the wet cold and was about to roll the window up again when she heard crying. At first she thought it must be a cat in distress, but the more she listened, the more human it sounded.

''That's a little child's voice!''

''You're right,'' he murmured, ''but where?''

Sensing a mystery, Chelsea opened her door to investigate. She could see a woman beckoning to them from across the road, shouting frantic cries for help.

By now Max had levered himself from the cab, their personal war put on hold in the face of this unexpected crisis. Chelsea chased after him. In case she couldn't get back to the station in time to report the story of Camille and the baby, maybe she'd find nuggets of a new drama unfolding here.

With arms flailing a panic-stricken young woman met Max halfway. Water ran down over her pretty features and dripped off her dark-blond braids. The rain had plastered her corduroy jumper against her thin body, revealing every shiver.

"Thank heaven y-you stopped!" she cried. "I need h-help!" Her hands gripped his hard-muscled forearms. "My baby girl wandered away from me and f-fell through some boards. I tried to go after her, but the framework is c-crumbling. I'm afraid to make a move or everything m-might cave in on top of her!"

Another trapped child.

As the sickness welled up in his throat, Max closed his eyes tightly for a moment.

Chelsea watched his reaction, stunned by the sudden pallor of his complexion, the way his body tensed. Something earthshaking was going on inside of him. But what?

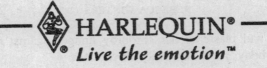

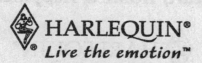

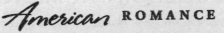
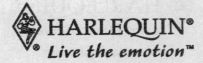

HARLEQUIN®
Super Romance®

...there's more to the story!

Superromance.
A *big* satisfying read about unforgettable
characters. Each month we offer *six* very different
stories that range from family drama to adventure
and mystery, from highly emotional stories to
romantic comedies—and much more! Stories
about people you'll believe in and care about.
Stories too compelling to put down....

Our authors are among today's *best* romance
writers. You'll find familiar names and talented
newcomers. Many of them are award winners—
and you'll see why!

If you want the biggest and best
in romance fiction, you'll get it
from Superromance!

Exciting, Emotional, Unexpected...

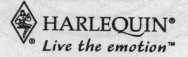

HARLEQUIN®
Live the emotion™

Harlequin® Historical
Historical Romantic Adventure!

*Imagine a time of chivalrous
knights and unconventional ladies,
roguish rakes and impetuous
heiresses, rugged cowboys
and spirited frontierswomen—
these rich and vivid tales will
capture your imagination!*

*Harlequin Historical . . .
they're too good to miss!*

HARLEQUIN®
INTRIGUE®

BREATHTAKING ROMANTIC SUSPENSE

Shared dangers and passions lead to electrifying
romance and heart-stopping suspense!

Every month, you'll meet six new heroes
who are guaranteed to make your spine tingle
and your pulse pound. With them you'll enter
into the exciting world of Harlequin Intrigue—
where your life is on the line
and so is your heart!

THAT'S INTRIGUE—
ROMANTIC SUSPENSE
AT ITS BEST!

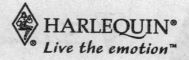

HARLEQUIN®
Live the emotion™

INTDIR06